T0121926

LYDIA

· · · · · · · · · · ·

Sandy J. Clark

Lydia

iUniverse books may be ordered through booksellers or by contacting:

iUniverse
1663 Liberty Drive
Bloomington, IN 47403
www.iuniverse.com
1-800-Authors (1-800-288-4677)

ISBN: 978-1-4502-5726-8 (sc)
ISBN: 978-1-4502-5724-4 (hc)
ISBN: 978-1-4502-5725-1 (e)

Print information available on the last page.

iUniverse rev. date: 11/19/2015

Dedication

This book is dedicated to my sister Charlene who inspired me to go ahead with my dreams of being a writer.
You have been by my side my whole life and helped me through the hard times and laughed with me in the good times. You truly are an angel that watches over me.

This is for you
I love you

The Story of Arachne

The word "arachnid" came from a Greek mythological tale told many years ago, and now I am going to tell the story to you.

Arachne was the daughter of a man named Idmon of Colophon in the city of Lydia. Lydia was famous for its splendid textiles and tapestries, so Arachne studied the art of weaving and became well-known for her work.

The nymphs would come from all over just to admire the beauty that was created from her loom. The nymphs asked Arachne one day if the goddess Minerva had blessed her with the gift of weaving. Arachne, being very arrogant, said that Minerva taught her nothing and then challenged Minerva to a contest to prove that she was the best weaver in the world. Arachne claimed to be better than the goddess, who was also a great weaver.

Minerva appeared in the disguise of an old woman and told Arachne that she should not compare herself to a goddess. Infuriated Arachne told the woman that she was better than Minerva could ever be.

Minerva then transformed herself into a beautiful woman in front of Arachne. Arachne taunted the goddess to take up the challenge, and Minerva did so.

Minerva wove a tapestry of images that told about the fate of humans who compared themselves to gods, and Arachne wove about the scandals and loves the gods were involved in and then put a border of ivy and flowers along the edges.

The goddess Envy judged the contest and proclaimed Arachne the winner. Minerva was outraged and physically beat Arachne, causing her to hang herself out of sheer terror.

Minerva, feeling remorseful, revived Arachne and turned her into a beautiful spider and turned the rope that she hung from into a web so that all the world could marvel at the beauty of Arachne's work for all eternity.

Prologue

The forest was unusually quiet, as if all the wildlife were hiding. In the distance, a waterfall with a fierce cold mass of water washed down the riverbanks, cleansing and wearing away everything in its path. The sun stretched its rays between the dense canopies of the rain forest, like playful fingers dancing on the mossy floor below. The air was thick with the musky fragrance of the dampened soil along with the sweet odor of the tropical foliage.

Titu strolled down the well-worn path that he had known since he was a child. He took in the sights around him. He gazed at the forest in complete awe, feeling the intensity of being a part of something bigger than him. His father and grandfather had taught him the ways of the shaman long before he could pronounce the names of the herbs he would collect every week for the elders. Titu would watch the elders for hours as they tirelessly ground and powdered roots and bark, producing remedy after remedy for their people. Not everyone was permitted to be a part of this process. Only the firstborn child to the shaman took on the privilege of carrying out the tradition.

Titu was now an elder with his own son to teach, but his son was not grasping herbalism. His son's frustration and lack of interest worried Titu. He needed someone to take his place once he passed on. The tribe depended on the shaman to take care of them and guide them in times of need.

Titu paused to gaze upon the delicate beauty of the Heliconia flower at his feet. Beside the flower grew the goal of his search, the Cinchona tree. Titu took out the knife that had been in his family for generations and began stripping small pieces of the bark away, trying not to damage the meat of the tree.

When he takes the bark back to the village, he will begin to prepare the juice by crushing the bark so that he can administer the medicine to his people in the hope it will cure the malaria that has struck his village.

Titu shook his head. *So many people, so little time.* The malaria has swept through the village so quickly, and, without the help of his son, the task seemed hopeless. As he continued to gather the bark, he placed it in his medicine bag. Once finished, Titu slowly stood up feeling the protest of his old bones.

"The journey back to the village will be slow," he muttered under his breath as he gazed at the tree and smiled. "I feel as old as you, but you will be here long after I am gone, old friend. Thank you for your gift."

He patted the pouch that now hung loosely on his hip. Leafcutter ants moved up and down the tree in a procession that seemed endless. Titu chuckled. "I know how you all feel. I have so much to do and very little time to do it. At least you have the help of your family to get the job done."

Titu turned and started his long journey home. After an hour of walking, his feet began to ache, and he decided to stop for a rest. He walked to the river, filled his flask, and splashed cool water on his neck. He leaned against a nearby tree to remove his moccasins and rub his swollen feet. There was a time when the walk back to the village seemed like a short, pleasurable stroll; now it took every ounce of energy Titu had.

There was a sudden rustling in the branches above his head, and he strained his neck to look up. It was probably a curious cockatoo mocking him for not having wings to ease his journey, he thought.

A gasp escaped his lips at the reality of what he saw, and he lost his footing and collapsed to the ground. He could hear the sickening crack of his hip as he landed on the jagged rocks of the riverbank.

Titu tried desperately to move, but the pain shot though his body. His sudden defenselessness crept up on him as he yelped like a wounded animal.

He could hear the thud of something suddenly dropping to the ground from the tree branches above him. Titu clawed at the ground, frantically dragging himself along the path as he felt the hairs on the back of his neck begin to rise. The thought of what might soon be his fate screamed in his mind.

The monstrous frame crept toward him, and Titu could taste his fear as the predator approached, but he could not conjure up the nerve to look behind him. Titu sorrowfully accepted what his ancestors felt should be his ill-timed demise. Trying to relax his body, he waited for what he knew would be a grim and agonizing departure.

A horrific scream was all that escaped his lips as the large razor-sharp fangs pierced into his old weathered skin just below the shoulder blades. His muscles began to spasm as his nervous system started shutting down. His last thought was of his people. He would not be able to help them. He felt guilt and shame at his failure.

Female wolf spiders carry their egg sacs behind them, attached to their spinnerets. When the spiders hatch, they crawl onto the mother's abdomen and hold on while she hunts. Around one week later, the babies molt to a larger size and then leave.

Chapter 1

The aggravating shrill of the phone disrupted the first peaceful sleep Marcus had been able to have in weeks.

He glanced at the clock, cursing. Who could possibly be calling at three o'clock on a Sunday morning? He clicked on the light that sat on the side table and clumsily fumbled for the phone.

He cleared his throat and then answered, not hiding his annoyance. "Hello?"

The man on the other end had a deep husky voice with a thick European accent. "Dr. Tolson, this is Dr. John Styne. I'm the emergency room MD with St. Jessica Hospital in Iquitos, Peru. I am sorry to call you at this hour, but I need your help. It's a matter of great urgency."

Surprise and intrigue filled his foggy mind as the last haze of sleep dissolved. He sat up and placed a pillow behind his back. He rubbed the sleep from his eyes. "What can I do for you, Dr. Styne?"

There was a pause. "We have had ten deaths within the villages in the last month. All the bodies have had mysterious bite marks on them. They look like spider bites, but the puncture wounds are a lot bigger and there is no sign of infection. There were minute traces of spider DNA in the bloodstream and highly toxic venom, so much so that the victims died within minutes. We don't have spiders of this type here."

Marcus's brow wrinkled, and he unconsciously chewed on his cheek. He didn't know when he started the habit but it seemed to help him concentrate, so he never quit.

"But there must have been something significant in the bloodstream."

Marcus grabbed the glass of water sitting on his bedside table and took a sip. "Could it be some tropical spider that you don't know about yet? Maybe it came from a shipment of some sort. That happens to us all the time." Questions were racing through his mind. He heard Dr. Styne sigh, and then there was another pause.

"We also found antigens of the falciparum malaria virus. We aren't sure if that was the cause of death because it usually takes up to three months to manifest. It doesn't look like the malaria had been in their systems that long. As for all the rest, I don't even want to venture a guess until you check it out." Styne sighed again, sounding defeated. "I am asking if you would be interested in assisting us on this. You have the expertise on this, and I could really use that right now, Dr. Tolson. This one is out of my league."

In his twenty-three-year career, he had never been asked to leave the country to work. He hadn't been back to Peru since he got his PhD in entomology from the university there. Then he branched off and specialized in arachnid biology. This was a big opportunity, but at what expense? He had obligations and bills to pay. He didn't have that kind of cash. Leaving New York on such short notice didn't give him much time to sort out his affairs. "That's a pretty tall order, Dr. Styne. It takes preparation."

Understanding what Marcus was trying to say, Styne countered. "I talked to the dean at the university. Do you remember Dean Joe Hursh?"

Marcus remembered the time he accidentally set fire to one of the labs and had to report to the dean's office. It was Marcus's turn to sigh; it was not one of the most flattering moments in his career.

"Yes, of course."

Styne continued. "The mayor is willing to pay all wages and travel expenses to get your team here. We are worried this thing is going to become an epidemic, and the mayor wants it dealt with ASAP." Dr. Styne's voice took on a tone of sarcasm. "He seems to think if it gets out to the press, we are going to have a decline in tourism. And god forbid if that happens."

Marcus smiled. "Well, how can I say no to the mayor?" he said with a chuckle, but Styne didn't join him in the amusement.

"We do need to get this controlled quickly though. People are—

how do you Americans say—dropping like flies? When is the earliest you can leave?"

"I will need to assemble my team. I can't do this alone, and it will take me a day or so to settle things here." Marcus got out of bed and walked down the hall to his study, taking the cordless phone with him. His desk was piled high with documents and charts from a few small projects he had been working on. He opened a drawer, found his Rolodex, and then sat down in the overstuffed office chair.

"Very well, we will set up accommodations and travel arrangements for you and your team. I will send you a fax with all the information you will need. I just need to know how many will be coming with you."

Marcus looked in his book and found the names of his field crew. "There will be four escorting me plus all our equipment."

"Very well, then I will have the plane tickets waiting for you at the airport. I will see you when you get here then. Thank you, Dr. Tolson. Have a good trip."

Marcus hung up the phone and let out a low whistle. He flipped through his file and found the names of his esteemed colleagues. At the top of the list was Vanessa Thompson, his top biologist and ex-girlfriend. They dated for two years before Marcus gave in to the ultimate fear of commitment. He picked up the phone and began to dial.

Groggily, Vanessa picked up at the other end, not bothering to look at the call display. "This better be good. I was in the middle of a hot dream with Keanu Reeves!"

Marcus stifled a comment. "Vanessa, it's Marcus."

Vanessa took in a quick breath, feeling flushed with embarrassment. She stumbled on her words. "Oh hey, Marc, I was just kidding."

With a smile, he said, "Yeah right, and I'm Betty Crocker."

Vanessa let out a jovial chuckle. "You always did look good in an apron. What on earth are you doing calling me at this godforsaken hour? I know it can't be to talk dirty to me. You never did that when we were together, so you sure as hell aren't going to do it now."

Marcus cringed at the stabbing remark but chose not to give Vanessa the satisfaction of knowing it got to him.

"Get packed. We're going to Peru."

. . . .

The flight to Peru was excruciatingly long, unbearably hot, and the food was lousy, but the flight attendants were beautiful, which made the trip a little less daunting. The flight attendant catering to Marcus had long auburn hair tied up in a French twist that was held in place with an exquisite barrette inlayed with rose quartz crystals. Her eyes were the deepest brown, and her lips were lusciously full, carefully lined with crimson red lipstick. Having her to look at made Marcus feel better about coming on this trip. He had forgotten how beautiful the women of Peru were.

As usual, Vanessa was chatting with the team about the migration of the Monarch butterfly. You never could keep her quiet for long, if at all. She was an integral bargaining chip at parties and fund-raisers; she kept conversations going, spirits high, and checks flowing with the financial bigwigs. She wasn't bad to look at, either, with her shoulder-length blonde hair that seemed to flow with every move she made. Her eyes were a shade of blue that could never be duplicated; it was like the color was specially made for only her. She moved with the grace of an angel and had the attitude of a pit bull. If there was something she wanted, she went after it with a vengeance.

Marcus didn't believe in the supernatural or anything close to it, but he had heard people talking in the past about how everyone has an aura, where colors seemed to float around a person and illuminate the room. Being the scientist that he was and out of pure curiosity, if nothing else, he had begun the experiment of looking at people a little more closely to see if he could invoke auras.

Marcus remembered watching Vanessa sleep, and he could have sworn he saw a glow around her pretty face. There were shades of blue and white so angelic, so soft, and Marcus found his feelings deepen with a love that made his heart soar. It took him by such surprise that he ended the relationship shortly after. Marcus reckoned if he could see that deeply into Vanessa, things had taken a serious turn that he wasn't ready for. With his heart screaming yes and his head saying quite the opposite, he made the hardest decision of his life and let her go. He knew he couldn't give her what she so very much deserved, so his conclusion seemed justifiable. Vanessa and Marcus agreed to disagree on a lot of things, and that was a great way to be in their profession.

The relationships he had before Vanessa were short but sweet. No heavy-duty feelings involved, just a good time at best. His parents divorced when he was young, so Marcus never really had a role model when it came to relationships. His mother never remarried, and his dad passed away a few years later in a horrific car accident. Vanessa, on the other hand, had two loving parents who had been together since elementary school and looked at Marcus as their future son-in-law. They even had a wedding gift picked out five months after they started dating. The breakup was just as hard on them as it was for Vanessa.

To this day, whenever their daughter comes for dinner, they have an extra setting at the table in the off chance he might come along. Marcus looked at Vanessa and his heart sank, suddenly feeling regret that no one had taken the time when he was younger to show him how to love or be loved or even just trust his heart.

Vanessa never quite understood why it all ended so abruptly. Marcus never talked about it much but said that he wanted to concentrate on his career. She knew that there was more to his words than he was ready to admit.

To Vanessa, their relationship now was a paradox, a balance of sorts, and their colleagues liked it that way.

They always said, "You make shitty lovers but a fabulous biology team." Although letting Marcus go wasn't what she wanted, she loved him enough to step away and let him work it out on his own. Through the years, there was always a profound nostalgic feeling between them.

Larry, who was Marcus's right-hand man on his entomology field team, doted on Vanessa's every move. He knew of the love she shared with Marcus, so he never showed his true feelings for her out of respect for his friend. He was a great entomologist but very unlucky in love. Larry had so much passion to offer and a heart of gold, but when it came to pursuing a woman, he was unable to follow through with his feelings. What he lacked in his love life he made up for in his work. He was passionate about his job, so much so that walking into his house was like walking into a bug zoo. He also felt that could be a big factor in why his relationships never worked out. Larry thought no woman in her right mind would venture into his house for fear of sitting on one of his precious bugs.

He was a good-looking man in his mid-forties, with a sturdy build, black hair graying at the temples, designer glasses, and a fabulous wardrobe. Larry was a man who knew how to dress like a millionaire on a poor man's budget.

Marcus reminisced about a time he had asked Larry to go for a drink after a tough day at work. It was one of those days where nothing went right and everyone was wrong. Larry accepted the invitation to meet at the local strip club around the corner later that night. Marcus was astonished when Larry came in. He was dressed to impress in a black three-piece suit complete with red tie, handkerchief, and black fedora. He was obviously in a prowling mood that was not expected by a dumbfounded Marcus.

"Larry! If I had known you wanted to get picked up I wouldn't have suggested a strip joint. I would have taken you to a place a little more respectable."

Larry took on a cavalier tone with a debonair look to match and spoke with a Sherlock Holmes accent. "Good man, what better place to pick up my next conquest! I can't possibly strike out here. As long as I have money in my pocket and a boner in my pants, I can't lose!"

Marcus laughed and choked on his drink. He patted Larry on the back and made a toast to what might never come. They drank into the night and ended up going home alone a couple hundred bucks shorter but had a great time doing it.

It had been a long time since Marcus had gone for a drink with anyone, let alone anyone on the team. He had been somewhat self-absorbed and followed in Larry's footsteps, exchanging a personal life for his work. His work took the majority of his time, and he had spread himself so thin that it didn't leave much room for social or personal ventures.

"Heads up!" From the corner of Marcus's eye, a flying breadstick veered off target, hitting him in the shoulder. Randy, who was Marcus's field researcher, yelled, "Hey, man, I am so sorry, my aim isn't so good. I was trying to get you in the head!" A snicker rang out from the team. "You were dreaming about the dragon queen again, I bet." They all looked at Vanessa.

With a raised middle finger and a disgusted look, she promptly replied, "Oh my god. How old are you? Besides, what the hell would you know, Randy? You couldn't get a date if you promised a girl gold instead of that pathetic, limp piece of wasted skin!" She pointed to the zipper of his faded blue jeans.

Randy was in his early thirties with streaked blond hair that was perfectly spiked at the top. He was fanatical about his hair; every strand had to be in its place. It was a year after he started with the team that they found out the majority of Randy's hair was surgically implanted due to massive hair loss caused by alopecia. His ego was all-consuming, and he thought he was the cream of the crop to every woman around him, a Casanova to the tenth degree. He entered into field research at the age of twenty-two because he didn't have the money to go all the way through to get his master's in biology. Although he came from a wealthy family, the late-night parties and immature fraternity antics swayed his father's decision to not fund his university degree. The team didn't have much respect for him; they just put up with him and accepted him as a misunderstood enigma.

Randy snickered. "I'm not nearly as bad as Cliff." He pointed in Cliff's direction and then broke into song.

> "Oh give me a home
> Where the pussies will roam
> And Cliff can't give it away.
> Where he beat his own meat
> And, oh, what a treat,
> He has to pay to get a good lay!"

His laughter was so loud the flight attendant gave him a stern look.

Vanessa turned to Randy with distaste written all over her face. "Did you come up with that all by yourself, or did your mama teach it to you?"

Cliff was a homely-looking fellow, twenty-four years old. He graduated at the top of his class. He had sunken green eyes, unruly red hair, permanent pockmarks on his face, and a scrawny little-boy figure. He was also a punching bag and scapegoat for all Randy's bad jokes.

Marcus piped up. "Okay, Randy, cool it. Leave the guy alone. We're almost at our destination. I suggest you all look over the paperwork I gave you at the office and catch up on what we are coming up against."

Randy turned around in his seat once again to look at Marcus. "Marcus, what's the deal with all this? Some natives get bitten and die. This doctor calls you from Peru and wants you to rush over there to investigate. Why? They can't handle a few little spider bites? What makes these cases so damn special that you have to fly halfway across the world to see it?"

"First off, there is no *I* in team. I do recall that there are five of us on this flight. Second, they haven't ever had a case like this before and decided to call in the best, and that, my friend, would be us."

Besides, you're being paid very well, so don't complain. Although, they have very good entomologists there. I guess they just want a second opinion."

Suddenly a male voice with a heavy Peruvian accent came over the loudspeaker. He began in Spanish and then again in English. "This is Captain Manuel Lafarge. In about thirty minutes, we will be landing in beautiful Peru. After we come to a complete stop, you will be exiting to the left of this aircraft. Your flight attendant will guide you when it is time. Please keep your seat belts fastened until the plane has come to a complete stop at the airport. On behalf of the flight staff and Peruvian Airways, we thank you for flying with us and bid you a good day."

Once the plane landed safely, the crew followed the crowd toward the main terminal of the airport.

As if the flight wasn't bad enough, the luggage department was even worse. Tourists from all over the world were piled into one spot trying to find their luggage. Family and friends who were picking them up scattered the lobby waving frantically to their loved ones. Some were flagging taxis down or getting on buses trying to get a ride to their hotels.

There was a quaint little lounge in the far left corner of the airport that seemed to be clear of everyone. Vanessa suggested the team go sit for a drink and let the craziness of the terminal pass.

Larry pulled a handkerchief out of his pants pocket and wiped his brow. "Hell yeah, I'm in for that. I know I could sure use a beer. This heat is unbearably hot. I don't know how people can live in this." Larry could feel the sweat dripping down his back and down to his belt. He prayed it wouldn't soak through his khaki-colored pants. *Not a good first impression to the locals,* he thought.

He assumed that if you live in the searing heat long enough you must get used to it, but who would want to?

Everyone picked up their carry-on bags and headed to the lounge.

There were big ceiling fans to circulate the air and portable fans sitting on the bar. They opted to sit at the bar next to the fans.

Marcus called the bartender over to put in their drink orders. "Perdóneme. Me gustaría cinco Coronas por favor." There was a tap on Marcus's shoulder. There stood a young woman with soft strands of brilliant red hair that cascaded down the length of her back. Her skin was freckled across the bridge of her nose, and her eyes were as green as the fields of Ireland where she grew up. She spoke with a slight accent, and when she smiled her dimples cupped the corners of her lips, keeping the smile protected from the cruel world that could cause her to frown.

"Excuse me, Dr. Tolson. My name is Joyce McGaver, and I am a senior student at Peru University. The dean sent me to pick up you and your team to bring you to the university lab. We have accommodations set up for you on the campus grounds." She looked into Marcus's eyes. Her heart skipped a beat as her lifelong goal was realized.

For her, what started as a hobby at the age of six turned into an obsession studying the things that people usually feared and took for granted. She was in her last year at the university working on her master's in entomology. Her parents always wanted her to become a doctor of medicine, and Joyce figured that this was close enough.

Marcus looked at the team with a smile and a raised eyebrow. "Well, how about that, guys? We have a ride." Turning back to the student patiently waiting, he said, "Let us grab our luggage, and then you can lead the way." He turned to the bartender again. "Cancele aquella orden, por favor."

Reluctantly, the team left their cold drinks behind and followed Marcus. They arrived in Iquitos by dusk, and the team was jet-lagged and hungry. The drive along the gravel road was beautiful. Big willow trees hung over the road so low you could almost touch them as you drove by. The sun beat down on Vanessa's face, and the breeze from the open window was blowing in her hair like hundreds of fingers caressing each strand.

The road gave way to an opening where the university stood in the midst of dozens of palm trees and lily bushes. The university grounds were at least forty acres with foliage in various places along makeshift stone paths leading to the main building and some splitting off to four sister buildings. There were oak benches in various spots all along the meticulously landscaped grounds overlooking the water where people could sit and study, eat lunch, or retreat to that favorite place in their mind and reflect.

A water fountain stood in front of the main building. In the middle of it sat a statue of a man holding a book in one arm, and the other arm stretched out as if to beckon someone.

No one really knew the significance of the statue except that it featured the man who built the university in 1869. The water shot up in a variety of heights around the man, and the cool spray called out to the team.

Marcus spoke with a tone of exhaustion. "Man, what I would give to put my big toe in that water right now." There was a grunt of agreement from the group. At the front of the entomology building, Larry noticed a banner at the top of the stairs that read, "Bienvenidos a la entomología laboratorio, donde aprendemos a bicho usted" (Welcome to the entomology laboratory, where we learn to bug you).

"Oh, aren't we a barrel of laughs." Larry turned to the group. "Does everyone have a dry sense of humor in Peru?"

Marcus snickered. "Where do you think I got mine?"

Randy, who was unusually quiet, looked at Cliff. "Gee, and I thought it was the lobotomy present he got at graduation."

Joyce stopped the SUV and the team stumbled out. Marcus leaned on the Land Rover. "And to think I thought I was just funny."

Vanessa turned toward the field in the front of the building where a few students were playing football. She smiled remembering her old university days, watching Marcus and his buddies throw the ball around on this same field. Vanessa and a bunch of girlfriends pretended to be the cheerleading squad. Vanessa smiled. It seemed so long ago.

"Look out!"

Vanessa was jolted back to reality in time to see the football coming directly at her. She instantly dropped her bag and extended her arms to catch the ball. It hit her with such force it knocked her flat.

A tall, handsome fellow ran to her aid and helped her up. "Wow, that was great! I can't believe you caught that."

Vanessa returned the ball, stood up, and rubbed her backside. "Yeah, well believe it. I have a bruise the size of Africa on my ass to prove it." They both laughed.

The student was now sizing up Vanessa in a way she knew all too well. He extended his hand. "I'm Taylor. Taylor Lemay." Vanessa took his hand and shook it firmly.

"Hi, Taylor, I'm Dr. Vanessa Thompson. I'm a biology professor and, no, I don't date students."

Taylor raised an eyebrow. "Not only can she catch a football, she's smart to boot." He winked at her.

Vanessa let go of his hand and felt the heat start at her toes and rise right to her face. She hated blushing; it was a dead giveaway to her loss of control.

The other guys on the field started shouting catcalls, and Taylor waved them off. "Well, I guess I better go. The natives are getting restless. Nice to meet you, Vanessa, I mean Dr. Thompson. Maybe I will see you around sometime." Before Vanessa could reply, he ran back to the field.

Vanessa turned to see the team looking at her with prying eyes.

Marcus had a mischievous grin. She passed by them with her hand up. "Talk to the hand, boys, talk to the hand."

They entered the university, and Joyce led the team to the boardroom to meet the dean and the elite group of student entomologists who had been working on the case for the last month.

Marcus stepped in first, and there was a hush in the room. Everyone stood up to greet the man about whom they had heard so much. Envy and admiration was apparent on all their faces as the dean stepped forward with an outstretched hand.

"Hello, Marcus, welcome back to the land of uncertainty." There was a grin on his face that Marcus clearly knew "It's been a long time."

Marcus put down his briefcase and shook the dean's hand.

Hursh smiled. "Way too long if you ask me."

"That it has been, Joe, that it has. How are your wife and kids? Jessica and Tammy must have their own kids by now, I would guess?"

The dean offered a chair to Marcus and the team and then sat down himself. "Yes, as a matter a fact, they do. Jessie is thirty-one and Tammy just turned twenty-four. They have given us three beautiful grandchildren. Debra is good too; she is vacationing in the Alps right now. The little ski bunny that she is."

Hursh suddenly remembered where he was and cleared his throat, embarrassed. "Well now, why don't you introduce me to your team?"

Marcus stood up and made a gesture to each member as he went around. "Well, Dean, this is Dr. Vanessa Thompson. She is my top biologist on staff." Vanessa tipped her head and said hello. "And this is Larry Schultz. He is my right-hand man in our entomology department." Larry tipped his head also in a polite gesture.

"Cliff Dacker here is Larry's second-in-command, so to speak. He is an entomologist of the finest breed. What can I say, I taught him everything he knows." Cliff sat up tall in his seat as if to make himself appear bigger than he was and raised his hand to give a quick wave. He looked at Randy with an impish grin. Randy just glared with a fiery viciousness that made Cliff's skin tingle.

"And then there is Randy Donavan, who you love to hate and hate to love." The look of surprise and confusion on Randy's face made Marcus inwardly chuckle knowing that he got the reaction he wanted. Every so often Randy needed to be put in his place, and everyone on the team knew Cliff didn't have the guts in him to do it, so Marcus did it for him. There was nothing Randy could do at that moment but smile through gritted teeth and muster a small chuckle too.

Marcus turned back to the dean. "To be fair and honest, I have to say he is a hard worker and is a quick study. I have to admit, without his expertise in the research department, I couldn't have gotten very far in my work." Looking at Randy with a contemptuous smile, he sat down.

Randy wasn't sure what to think, so he chose to ignore the comment. In the corner of his eye he saw Cliff stifle a laugh. He looked as if he wanted to say something so bad he would spontaneously self-combust if he held it any longer.

Dean Hursh slapped his hand on the table and everyone jumped. "All right, then I guess that does it for the pleasantries. This is Dr. John Styne. I believe you talked on the phone a few days ago. He is the professor of the biology lab and also a fine doctor at the hospital in town. These fine specimens in the white jackets are the team we put together for this case, most of which are in the last term here and are close to being on their way to the wild jungle of entomology. I thought it would be good for them to be involved in something like this, to give them a taste of what it is going to be like out there in the world."

Marcus's first gut feeling about this idea was unpleasant at best. "With all due respect, Dean, don't you think this is a little advanced? I mean we don't even know what the hell we are dealing with yet. I really don't think they are ready for this."

The dean smiled at Marcus. For as long as Dean Hursh had known Marcus, his lack of respect for authority had never diminished. "Marcus, don't worry, they have been working on this for a month now. They can help get you up to speed on things." The gut feeling in Marcus's stomach got worse, but he was smart enough to know not to press the issue right then.

Dean Hursh slapped the table once more and stood up. "I will leave you all to it then. I will be in my office if you need me further." With that he walked over to Marcus again, shook his hand, leaned over, and whispered in his ear. "Come over to the house later for a drink. We have a lot of catching up to do, my friend." He then smiled and said good-bye.

Dr. Styne flicked on the light to the slide projector and turned off the overhead lights.

"Let's get right down to it then. I have taken some video footage of the victims in question. These villagers were brought to me at the hospital. The first victim came in on August 5."

He changed slides in the projector. "He is a member of the Quichua people from deep in the Amazon. He had multiple abrasions all over his body. If you look here on his left shoulder, there is one spider bite. There were traces of neurotoxins found in his bloodstream and major organs, and there were clues he may have had the beginning signs of malaria. There were traces of venom and Atrax toxins found as well. Malaria, as you know, is contracted through mosquito bites, not spider bites. The morgue filed the cause of death as malaria-related, but things just didn't add up. There are ten in total, including the shaman of the tribe. He had similar injuries. The morgue concluded that he had a broken hip and femur due to a possible fall. He was in his eighties, so I would imagine there wouldn't be a fight. He had a pouch full of fresh Cinchona bark, which villagers use for medicine to treat malaria. They never use traditional medicines. They rely heavily on their shaman. He must have been treating his village before he died."

The doctor made a gesture toward the students. "We have been working closely with Dr. Jim Dunstan, and we were instructed to call you, Dr. Tolson."

Jim Dunstan stood up now. He was a very distinguished-looking man with a square jawline that was set in a serious look. His eyes were of the softest aqua blue with black borders as if to keep the waters within. His thin mustache was trimmed ever so neatly. His jet black hair was parted on the left side and cropped short like a corporate executive. He wore a white lab coat, but Vanessa could tell just by looking at him that he took very good care of his body. His burly chest and ripped arms held an air of confidence that made Vanessa's toes curl. She found herself hanging on every word that his deep husky Peruvian voice produced.

"Hola. Hello. Thank you for coming all this way to join our little soiree. We would never have called you in if we thought we could figure out this damn thing on our own. I would be the first person to admit I need help, and that time is now. I have hit a brick wall on this one, and so far all we know is it's a spider that is not native to Peru, possibly a Sydney funnel-web spider. Second, the malaria is the same from one victim to the next, but there are varying components within the bloodstream that lead us to believe they not only had malaria for approximately one week before they died but had also succumbed to the venom of a spider. For the amount of bodies we are getting, there would have to be a home close to the tribe's village, but nothing was found. The funnel-web spider is native to Australia, not here. They don't like the dampness of the rain forest. It's almost like the spider is searching for something, but the victims are unsuitable due to the malaria. We sent a medical team to the villages to treat the rest of the tribe for the malaria, seeing that they no longer have their shaman, but that in itself has been a struggle. They don't want our help."

Vanessa let out a perplexing sigh. "Wait a minute, I'm a little confused here. You say it could be a Sydney funnel-web spider. How could it have gotten here?"

Jim Dunstan frowned. "I don't know, but that's not all we found. We found traces of a few different species in the bloodstream. So unless the villagers got ganged up on by more than one spider, which is very unlikely, I would have to say it is only one type of spider that is sticking close to the village."

Vanessa put her hands to her head and took a deep breath. "Are you trying to tell us we have some sort of unstable mutant spider on our hands that is on a vendetta? How insane does that sound?"

Jim gave Vanessa a look that attempted to encase her soul. The gaze only lasted a second, but to Vanessa it was an eternity of warmth and seduction. She suddenly felt her body react as she adjusted herself on her seat. There was a game of intrigue starting that made her slightly uncomfortable but captivated. She thought to herself, *Stop it, Vanessa, this is neither the time nor the place!*

"Your guess is as good as mine, Dr. Thompson. But in a nutshell, yes, that is precisely what I am saying." Jim winked.

She reached a shaky hand to the glass of water that was in front of her as Jim turned back to Marcus. "Any thoughts would be greatly appreciated, Dr. Tolson."

Marcus watched the whole courting scene between Vanessa and Jim and had a few exasperated thoughts on it. But this was business, and he had to keep his head on his shoulders. He put on his best game face. "I would like to know what other evidence you found that leads you to believe it's a new species of arachnid. Plus, if the villagers are so standoffish to outsiders, how did you find out about the problem in the first place?"

Jim gathered his notes. "First off, there was a team of botanists studying the foliage in the area when they came across the village. They sent a team member back to get help. As for the second question, the sizes of the fang marks for one thing are far larger than a funnel-web spider. I would say it is more tarantula, but it pierced the skin like a knife through butter, similar to a Sydney funnel-web. As you are aware, a funnel-web spider can go through a toenail quite easily but would have to be pulled out to dislodge it. It would have to be a much larger size to remove itself." He cleared his throat again. "We also found the active compound Tx2-6."

Larry let out a snicker. "Are you serious! This is beautiful."

Vanessa turned to him with a raised brow. "Care to explain?"

Larry looked at Jim. "May I?" Jim graciously gave Larry the stage, thankful for the interruption.

"Well, Tx2-6 is a compound or short protein. It increases the nitric oxide levels within the main cylinders in the penis of humans and primates, causing a very large and painful erection that lasts for hours. Scientists are now using it in Viagra pills to help men with erectile dysfunction. But mix that with the effects of the Sydney funnel-web and you are looking at an extremely painful and cruel death. The funnel-web spider, on the other hand, has venom called Atrax toxin, like Dr. Styne mentioned. That is a whole other ball of wax. The toxin reaches the circulatory system very quickly. If it is not treated immediately, it will kill a person in fifteen minutes. The fatal blow is respiratory distress and cardiac arrest resulting in death."

Jim smiled and continued. "So as you can see we have quite a problem on our hands. I have printed copies of our findings in the file in front of you."

Marcus thought for a moment. "Okay, why don't we sleep on it and rejoin in the morning after we have had a chance to read the material? Let's say 7:00 am?"

"That would be fine." Jim turned to Joyce. "Joyce, can you show Dr. Tolson and his team to their rooms, please?"

Joyce nodded eagerly, standing up. Jim turned again to Marcus. "Your luggage has been brought up already, I believe."

Standing up and grabbing the files off the table, Marcus began walking to the door. Vanessa tapped him on the shoulder. "Marc, are you all right?"

Marcus didn't even turn around but replied through gritted teeth. "Yeah, I'm fine. Just tired." And he kept walking down the hall to his room.

Vanessa got an uneasy feeling, like ice-cold fingers reaching out to grab her. Slowly looking over her shoulder, she caught a glimpse of Jim behind her five feet away talking to Cliff. She held her breath as their eyes met. He smiled and winked once again. Vanessa fumbled to hold the papers that were in her hand and then walked down the hall toward her room thinking, *Why does he seem so familiar?*

The Goliath bird-eater tarantula can be as big as a dinner plate and can snatch birds from their nests. The smallest spider is a mygalomorph spider. Its body is the size of a pinhead.

Chapter 2

It was a barely audible knock on the door at 6:00 am, and Marcus wasn't even sure if that was what he was hearing. The door opened a crack, and Vanessa walked in quietly to kneel at the side of the bed. Marcus didn't even have to open an eye to know who it was. He could smell the sweet mixture of jasmine, sandalwood, neroli, and patchouli and was taken back to a time when they were still dating. He liked to smell her delightful scents, the smell of her skin right after making love. He suddenly felt her fingertips brush across his face. He decided to pretend he was still asleep to see what she would do.

Vanessa felt the coolness of Marcus's skin on her hand and felt a yearning for his body against hers. She remembered how lovemaking was first thing in the morning: the playfulness of their love, the showers together, dressing each other for work and then undressing each other. She wanted to crawl into bed with him right then and there. But she knew that it was over between them and couldn't jeopardize their work ethic. That was a long time ago, and Marcus had moved on, dating again not long after.

As if Marcus had read her mind, he gently whispered, "Lock the door and come keep me warm." Vanessa jumped and all at once felt embarrassed, angry, and turned on.

"I thought you were asleep! You scared me half to death." Marcus opened his eyes and put his hand to her cheek, feeling the softness over her skin. He instantly felt his body respond. "You know how I am in the morning, baby. I'm hoping you came to give me a special good morning."

Vanessa looked down and saw the sheets move. Eyebrow raised, she thought to herself, *Well, at least I still have an effect on him.* Not wanting him to see that it was affecting *her* too, she slapped him on the arm and stood up. "I just didn't want you to be late, so you better get up and get in the shower, Marc."

Grabbing his member he looked down saying loud enough for Vanessa to hear, "Well, buddy, I guess it's another lonely morning."

Vanessa felt the wetness between her legs, her body heat rising. She loved the way he touched himself. Turning away flustered, she walked to the door. "See you in the lab. I'll leave you and the Palmer sister alone."

Closing the door behind her, she leaned on it and muttered under her breath, "That makes the two of us alone this morning." With a sigh, she walked toward the lab.

Larry was already looking at specimens and charts long before anyone got out of bed that morning. He couldn't sleep thinking about a possible new species that he didn't know about yet. He wanted to know everything about it, and he was becoming somewhat obsessed.

Vanessa walked in to find him looking through a microscope, fiercely turning the dials and then looking back at some charts with the look of determination on his face like a mad scientist. He didn't even hear her enter the lab. The shock of finding someone standing next to him when he turned around made him suddenly jump back, hitting the table and sending its contents tumbling to the cement floor. Glass from the petri dish shattered and flew in all directions; the lens of the microscope cracked as it was sent sailing across the room.

Vanessa dropped to her knees to try to retrieve the articles. "Oh shit! Larry, I am so sorry. I didn't mean to sneak up on you like that." Without looking, she reached for some of the dish and a sharp pain struck her like a lightning bolt as the glass cut through the skin of her finger.

Vanessa recoiled her hand clutching it to her bosom. "Ouch, son of a bitch!" The blood slowly trickled down her hand. "I haven't had my coffee yet. That's my problem."

Larry grabbed a paper towel from a nearby sink and wrapped it around Vanessa's finger. "Don't you worry about this. I can clean it up. You go get us a cup of coffee in the lounge. I hear it's pretty good here."

"But I—"

"Go, get, scram."

Larry shooed Vanessa with a sweep of his hand and went back to cleaning. Feeling defeated, Vanessa stood up and walked out of the room. Larry grabbed a broom and mop and, after picking up all the big pieces, he began to sweep up the little stuff.

Cliff came through the door with a coffee in one hand and a bagel in the other. "Hey, Larry, not a great start to the morning, I see." With a cheesy smile, he sat down on one of the stools in front of Larry. "Do you want some help, buddy?"

Larry turned to face Cliff and chuckled. "No, I can manage. I hope this doesn't come out of my salary."

"What happened?" Taking a bite of his bagel, Cliff scanned the floor for any more broken glass.

"Vanessa came in and I didn't hear her. She scared the living shit out of me, and I bumped into the table and things went flying. I guess I was really into what I was doing." Wringing out the mop, he then placed it in the closet. Satisfied that he had gotten all the remnants of glass, Larry pulled up a stool and sat next to Cliff.

Cliff swallowed a piece of bagel and then drank some coffee to wash it down, waiting for his teammate to continue, but nothing was said.

Marcus walked through the door to meet two stone-faced men looking back at him. "Good morning, gentlemen, you're here early."

Larry responded with a snort, "I have been here for a couple hours already. I couldn't sleep, so I came to see what I could find out."

Marcus looked as if he was about to laugh and teasingly said to Cliff, "Leave it to Larry to beat us to the punch." Then to Larry he said, "Did you find anything you would like to share?"

Larry looked at the floor where the destroyed microscope used to be. "Well, I may have, but I had a little mishap. But I can get it all together again in no time."

Marcus looked confused. "Mishap?"

Cliff jumped into the conversation now and put his hand on Marcus's shoulder. "Don't bother asking."

Vanessa returned with three cups of hot coffee and a bandage on her finger. Placing a coffee on the table for Larry and handing another to Marcus, she said her good mornings and proceeded to a desk at the corner of the room. She flipped through the folders that were in front of her and started writing some notes.

Randy stumbled into the room, briefcase in hand and a shit-eating grin on his face. Everyone looked at him with surprise at the fact that it wasn't even nine in the morning and he was awake. "Good morning, fellow teammates! Lovely day, isn't it?" Placing his briefcase on the floor next to his new station, he blew Vanessa a kiss.

Vanessa retorted with her bandaged middle finger. This was her usual greeting for him every morning. With disgust she replied, "I can't believe we have only been here a few hours and *you* got yourself laid."

Randy's face contorted with a surprised smirk. "How the hell did you know that? I didn't have time to tell anyone yet."

Vanessa jeered. "How the hell could I not know, you pig? My room is next to yours. I *heard* you all damn night long!" She did her best bimbo impression. "Oh, Randy! Babe, oh yeah, like that. Fuck me, you stud!" Vanessa forced a gagging sound. "It was enough to make me sick!"

Randy looked down at Vanessa's bandaged finger. "Maybe if you gave your fingers a break and get a real man."

"My fingers do just fine, and they don't talk back or give me any grief like you." Marcus grinned from ear to ear thinking to himself, *So that is why I got a morning visit. She was horny as hell. Maybe if I had pressed the issue a little more she would have given in pretty easily.* He muttered under his breath, "Damn it, I could have gotten lucky!" Shrugging it off, he went to his desk and sat down.

The rest of the team began bringing in their equipment and proceeded to delegate the tasks that needed to be done. A few hours went by and no one seemed to notice. By eleven o'clock Larry's stomach began to growl and he realized he hadn't eaten yet, so he announced that he was going to go to the cafeteria. Vanessa and Marcus put in their order and then went back to work as Larry left the room. There were students of all ages in the halls trying to get to their classrooms, pushing and shoving and yelling to their friends as they proceeded down the narrow walkways.

A Nerf ball flew past Larry just inches from his head, causing him to remember why he was glad the school years for him were over. In his day he was considered a geek with a microscope as a best friend. He would get picked on from other students and made an example of by the teachers. Girls liked him for the homework he would willingly do for them just so he could have some contact with the feminine gene pool. It was not a time he would choose to go back to.

A student jumped in the air to catch the football but in the process hip-checked Larry and threw him into the wall.

Regaining his composure, Larry turned to retaliate but abruptly stopped, noticing it was the same student that Vanessa had encountered the day before.

"Hey, man, I'm really sorry about that. Are you okay?" Taylor asked out of politeness and not real concern as he threw the ball back to his buddy.

Larry spat back in annoyance, "You know, one of these days you are going to really hurt someone and you had better hope the guy isn't bigger than you or you will get a real shit kickin!"

Taylor laughed and began walking away, hollering over his shoulder, "Yeah, whatever, pops. You have a good day too."

Larry shook his head and cursed under his breath as he entered the cafeteria and ordered what was on his list. A few minutes later he was on his way back to the lab with paper bag and coffee in hand. But this time he decided to walk the long way through the garden outside.

The smells of fresh flowers were abundant in the air. The sun was shining down on Larry's face, and the warmth of it was inviting him to stay in the garden for just a little while. *Sitting on the bench for just a minute won't hurt too much,* Larry thought to himself. He could smell the ocean in the light breeze and hear the birds calling to their mates. He figured that this was what paradise was all about.

Suddenly an eerie quiet fell over the garden, and Larry felt icy tendrils of a presence that was not wanted, like an unseen predator was watching nearby. Larry's heart began to race. He turned to look around but could see nothing. Feeling vulnerable, he stood up, quickly walked away, and ducked into the building.

On the back of the bench where Larry sat was the undetected visitor only inches away from where Larry's shoulder was. Eight pairs of eyes lurked, watching its opportunity walk into the stone structure.

Most spiders have eight eyes, but some have no eyes, and others have as many as twelve eyes. Most can detect only between light and dark, while others have well-developed vision. All spiders have highly evolved systems to detect prey and danger.

Chapter 3

Marcus stood in front of Dean Hursh's office and introduced himself to a very butch older—much older—receptionist. As a matter of fact, she looked like a prison guard on a bad-hair day.

"Hello, Dr. Tolson. Have a seat and I will tell the dean you are here. Would you like a coffee while you are waiting?"

Marcus found a seat and put his briefcase down. "No, thank you. I think I will survive without any more this morning, but I could sure use a scotch on the rocks with one of those little umbrellas." With a little chuckle he sat down.

It was obvious the secretary didn't find his dry sense of humor all that funny. She had pursed lips into a frown that all but swallowed her mouth. Her beady eyes bore a hole right through Marcus, and he found himself, feeling like a child in trouble, sinking down into his seat. The woman turned on her heels and marched down the hall.

A moment later he was in Hursh's office with the secretary guarding the door. "That will be all, Gertrude, thank you." Hursh stood up to relieve the woman of what she thought were her duties.

The door closed and Marcus began to relax. "Holy shit, Joe. Quick, poke my eyes out. I don't ever want to see that again! Where the hell did you get *her?* She could scare the fur off a billy goat!" Marcus shook like he just caught a chill. "I don't think I will ever have a good sex life again!"

"Well, she isn't much to look at but she is a damn good secretary. Besides, my wife would never stand me having a good-looking woman in the office, but I can send Gertrude over to your room and get her to teach you the facts of life, if you want."

Marcus's eyes opened wide, and his body slightly convulsed at the thought of having that woman (if she was a woman at all) in his bed.

"Ah, no thank you. I do just fine on my own."

Hursh picked up his coffee cup and took a sip. "So what do I owe the pleasure of your visit?"

Marcus opened his briefcase. "Well, I wanted to know a few things. We didn't really get time to talk last night."

"Shoot, I'll help you as best I can, Marcus." He put his cup down again. Marcus went right to the punch.

"Do you still have the bodies in the morgue? I wanted to take a look myself to see if I can come up with anything else to go on."

Hursh leaned back in his chair and gave a low whistle. "Damn, no I don't, Marcus. One of the bodies that came in was the tribe's medicine man. It had to be returned right after the autopsy. The rest of the bodies had to be sent back to the village as well. We collected all the data I thought we needed. They have a special ritual they have to do to honor their dead leader. Something to do with releasing his soul to move on to a higher plain, yada, yada, yada. Something like that, so I couldn't get in the way of that. It would be somewhat sacrilegious, wouldn't it? I don't need a lawsuit, let alone bad karma. We were really pushing our luck doing the autopsy." A broad smile set on his face.

Marcus smiled too. "Who was the first one to examine the bodies?"

Hursh tapped a pen on the table in thought. "I believe it was Jim Dunstan, but I can't be sure without looking at the files. It would only make sense though. He is the first-in-command, so to speak."

Marcus looked confused. "I thought you were."

"I just oversee everyone in the department. I don't get my hands dirty in the trenches anymore."

Hursh stood up, walked over to the coffeemaker, and refilled his cup, offering a cup to Marcus. Marcus politely declined. He felt that something wasn't quite right about Jim Dunstan, and he had felt it first in the boardroom the night before at the meeting. He couldn't put a finger on it, but he knew something about Jim wasn't adding up. "Do you know if he did the examination alone?"

Dean Hursh turned around to look at Marcus. "That I couldn't tell you, as I don't know. What are you getting at, Marcus?"

Marcus shrugged his shoulders. "Nothing, I just want to get all the facts."

Hursh sat back down and looked at Marcus. "Sounds to me like there is more to this than you are willing to tell me. You don't trust him, do you?"

Marcus shifted in his seat. "Well, I can't say I get a good feeling from him, to be completely honest, Joe. But I just met the man, so I don't want to say too much."

Hursh thought for a moment, tapping the desk again. "Actually, Marcus, you have met him before. He was in your grad class when you attended this university. He was the one who told Styne to call you." Hursh paused. "Jim has worked with us for some time now, and we haven't had any problems so far." He paused. "Not that I know of anyway."

Marcus looked like someone had slapped him. He looked out the window of the office, not sure what to say and selecting his words as he went. "I don't remember him. That was a long time ago. Would you mind if I looked at Dunstan's file? I'm not judging your ability to hire qualified people or anything like that; I am just curious to see his credentials."

Hursh smiled. "You know they are strictly confidential, Marcus. I can't just hand them over to someone. But I can tell you that he has great credentials. He has worked for a few upstanding companies as well as some well-established schools."

Marcus nodded. "I'm sure he did. I totally understand you don't want to go against strict policies. I just thought it would give me a better understanding of who I am working with."

Hursh thought for a moment in consideration of Marcus's request. Opening his desk drawer he retrieved a set of keys and then stood up. He walked to his filing cabinet and unlocked it, sliding the second drawer open. Finding what he was looking for, Dean Hursh turned back toward Marcus and sat on the edge of his desk with the file in his hand.

"I am going to put this file down and walk away. If anyone asks me I will deny ever knowing what happened to it. I will say I must have forgotten to lock my office. Do you understand?"

Marcus looked at Hursh with a stunned gaze. Only one word escaped his lips. "Completely."

The fisher, or raft, spider is able to walk across the surface of a body of water by skating like a water strider. When it detects prey, like insects or tiny fish under the surface, it can quickly dive to capture its dinner.

Chapter 4

The local students' favorite bar was only a few miles from the campus in Chiclayo, so on most nights students, as well as teachers, could be found there drowning their sorrows concerning overdue papers, bad grades, and broken relationships.

It was unusually quiet for some reason, but Jim felt a calm come over him when he walked in. He smiled to himself at the thought of being able to drink his beer without hearing the rowdiness of the students.

He paid for his drink and then sat at a table in the corner. An hour went by, and four beers later no one had walked into the peaceful bar. Jim was about to stand up to leave when the door suddenly swung open.

A beautiful woman walked in with an air of confidence that stunned Jim into sitting down quickly. She was wearing a black sarong with a bright yellow tank top that tied at the waist so it showed her flat tanned belly complete with belly button jewelry. Her hair was a mass of jet black ringlets that flowed halfway down her back, flowing behind her as she walked to the bar. Her bangs came just below her eyebrows and hung ever so slightly over her deep brown eyes, like a curtain trying to hide her soul.

Jim's heart began to beat faster and his mouth became as dry as the Mojave Desert. He surrendered to her beauty, completely mesmerized, and the blood pumped faster through his veins. His groin ached as his pants grew taut, but Jim didn't seem to notice. He watched every move she was making as she walked to the jukebox, inserted the appropriate coins, and then carefully selected a couple of songs.

The music filled the air with a soft melody as she closed her eyes and began to move with an erotic, sensual swaying motion that made Jim squirm in his seat. He wanted her, needed her to fill his desire. He continued to watch in awe of her beauty and started to get up to talk to her when the door swung open again and a bunch of students flooded the room whooping and hollering.

Jim sat back down in frustration. It was obvious they had already started drinking and came to raise some hell. There had been a Peru University football game that night and, by the looks of the students, they had won.

Jim scanned the group and noticed that some of them were from his biology class. He also knew they were trouble. Two in particular were Taylor Lemay and Bobby Roe, a couple of football scholarship yuppies who had nothing better to do than make other students' lives rough.

They got into biology to make their parents happy but had no interest in the field. Taylor was well-known as a lady's man who had a bit of a rap sheet. He was accused of date rape at the end of the last term, but the charges were dropped before it went to trial.

Bobby Roe was one of those big, stupid, captain of the football team sidekicks. He followed Taylor around like a puppy in hopes that girls would fall all over him like they did for Taylor.

Taylor noticed the raven-haired beauty and made his advance, and Jim cringed when he realized he had been beaten to the punch. He took a long swig of his beer and reluctantly watched the scene unfold in front of him.

Coming up behind her, Taylor placed his hand on her soft shoulder, and she jumped and swung around with big frightened eyes looking back at him. Taylor jumped back at the force of it all. "Hey, hold up! I just wanted to come over and say hello and introduce myself."

She relaxed a little and smiled. "Oh, I'm sorry. I'm not usually this jumpy, but with the rumors that have been going around lately about a serial killer and rapist, who could blame me?" She took a sip of her drink. Then she added, "I don't know why I would think anyone would come in here and kill me in front of witnesses." She laughed, and it emanated across the room, making Taylor shiver as it reverberated off every nerve in his body. He did not realize that the beauty in front of him noticed his reaction. She looked at him with a contorted half-smile. "Are you okay?"

"Ah, yeah, I'm fine. You know I have to tell you, baby, you are the greatest." Giving a low whistle, he continued. "Man, you make my knees weak."

Surprised by his answer, she chuckled and replied, "Really now? Like I'm supposed to believe that pickup line."

Thinking fast, he countered, "No, I guess not. You're much too smart for that one. Would you like to dance with me and make me the envy of the room?" Proud of what just came out of his mouth, he gave a cocky smile.

She gave him a once-over. "Well, you sure have an interesting way of picking up women. I have to admit I haven't heard that line before, so I think it's worth one dance. My name is Shyla Demone." She graciously put her hand out to shake his.

To her tantalizing surprise, he took her hand, grabbed the drink in her other hand with his free hand, placed it on the bar table, and then gracefully swung her onto the dance floor.

They swayed to the music as if they had done it many times before. Little did she know they would be dancing many more times that evening. Jim Dunstan sat watching, his anger building as he guzzled he drink. He ordered another and waited.

The design in the web of the orb-weaving spiders serves a variety of purposes. It can be a warning for birds so they don't fly into the web, and it attracts insects to fly into it on purpose. The umbrella shape shades the spider from the hot sun.

Chapter 5

The team sat talking in the boardroom while they waited for Marcus to show up. Not much had gotten accomplished in the last few days other than a complete understanding that they were not dealing with a normal everyday spider. Randy tapped his pencil on the table impatiently. "Where the hell is Marcus?" Then taking his sunglasses off and rubbing his eyes, he said, "Not like we don't have other things to do right now."

Vanessa yawned, put her feet up on the table, leaned back, placed her hands behind her head, and closed her eyes. "Sorry to throw a wrench into your plans, but he is the boss, dumbass. Why don't you just sit back and soak all of this in? We're in Peru, for Christ's sake, so don't start whining, bitching, and complaining." She sighed. "When this is all done I am going to a private beach somewhere to do some serious tanning."

Randy sat up in his seat and licked his lips. "Can I come and watch, please? I promise I will be a good little boy."

Vanessa snorted. "Not bloody likely, reptilian boy! Maybe I will find myself a hunky Peruvian man to put some suntan oil on my back."

Randy almost drooled on his shirt at the thought of Vanessa being naked in the hot sun with glistening oil all over her luscious body. As if on cue, Marcus walked into the room, files in one hand and a coffee in the other.

"So how goes the battle troop? Find anything I should know about?"

Larry put his hands up in the air in an attempt to look defeated. "Nothing yet. I personally would like to take a trip to where the bodies were found and see what we can come up with there. Maybe we can find some valuable clues."

Marcus sat down and mulled it over for a moment. "You might have a point, Larry. Get the team ready. You can leave in the morning. Vanessa, I would like you to stay here with me. I may need your help."

Vanessa glared at him with a defiance that left Marcus feeling uneasy. He knew how much she enjoyed doing fieldwork, but he wanted to keep her safe, even if that meant keeping her at the university with him. The tension was thick, and no one said a word.

Cliff shifted in his seat and then stammered, "Umm … Marcus, who do you want to go? I mean Randy should go because, well, research is his thing. Larry, I think, is chomping at the bit to go and well … I … I don't mean to be forthright, but you don't need two entomologists on the scene, do you?"

Marcus snickered. "Are you trying to tell me you have no interest in going?"

Cliff looked down at the table away from Marcus's gaze. "I just thought I might be needed more here. I could do more analysis on the blood samples."

Randy laughed out loud. "You're nothing but a chicken shit. You're afraid of what we might find out there," he snorted. "Some entomologist you are."

Cliff was abruptly thrown back to a time as a child when his older brother used Cliff's fears for his own sick and twisted fun.

He was seven years old, and his brother, Ted, was ten. Their mother was making a special dinner that night for their father, who had just gotten a promotion from salesman to assistant manager of the local realty office. She asked Cliff to go in the basement to retrieve a jar of the dill pickles she had canned in the spring. They were their father's favorite, and she wanted everything to be perfect right down to the neatly folded napkins.

"Tonight is your father's big night, Cliffy, so help me and be a good boy. Go downstairs for me, would you, doll?"

Cliff hated the basement and rarely went anywhere near it. He hated the musky smell of dampness and the constant drip of the washbasin. The overhead light was old and rusted, barely giving enough light to see a foot past your own nose, and Cliff could have sworn he heard rats squeaking in every corner of the big dark room. The thought of a beady-eyed rodent running across his feet made him squirm and shiver. He slowly walked down the old wooden stairs, and they groaned under the pressure of his weight, which was only a mere sixty pounds. The room felt like it was closing in on him, and he fought the urge to turn and run back up to the safety of his bedroom. Putting one foot in front of the other, Cliff walked across the room to the shelf that contained all the canned goods and jars of pickled carrots, beets, asparagus, and dills. His mother loved to make her own canned goods.

It helped considerably when the money got tight, but now they wouldn't have to worry, thanks to his father's promotion. Things were starting to look up for the Dacker family.

There was a noise behind Cliff, and he jumped a foot as Ted grabbed him by the shoulder. "Hey, goof, what's taking you so long? Mom was starting to wonder if the boogie man got you down here."

Cliff slapped Ted's hand away. "There is no such thing as a boogie man, stupid."

Ted's malicious smile spread like an infectious disease. "Oh, really? I guess Dad never told you about what happened to the last kid that lived here before we moved in."

Cliff picked up the jar of pickles. "Shut up, Ted! You're just trying to scare me, and it won't work." Even as he said the words he knew it was a lie. He was scared stiff.

Ted laughed. "Then why do you look like you are going to pee in your pants?" He looked over at the old refrigerator they had that belonged to their grandmother when she was alive. It was yellowed after years of being in the basement, and the old pull-down leaver was rusted in the upright position. "Maybe I'll just lock you in Grandma's fridge and tell Mom that you disappeared."

Cliff went to turn and go back up the stairs, ignoring his brother, but Ted grabbed his arm. Cliff's breath caught in his throat. Oh god, no, he can't be serious.

Ted clamped his hand over Cliff's mouth so that he couldn't scream and wrestled him to the waiting fridge. The jar of pickles fell to the floor and smashed on the cement as Cliff fought with every fiber of his being, but his brother had a foot of height and ten pounds to his advantage. Ted punched Cliff in the stomach causing him to lurch forward and gasp for air, which gave Ted enough time to let go of one hand to open the door and get Cliff in the fridge. Coming to his senses, Cliff jammed his foot against the door. "Ted, stop it! This isn't funny!"

Ted gave one good shove, and the door slammed shut and the lock engaged with a snap. Ted could barely hear the terrified screams of the little boy and wondered if maybe he had taken the joke a little too far.

If his parents found out he would be in severe trouble and then he wouldn't be able to order the Vertibird he saw on the back of his comic book. Having second thoughts he figured he better let Cliff out and clam him down. He would have to threaten him to get him to keep his mouth shut so he wouldn't get caught.

Ted pulled on the old door but the door didn't open. He pulled harder but nothing happened, and he suddenly realized the door was stuck. Panic began to rise at the seriousness of the situation. "Cliff, the door won't open! Start kicking it."

Cliff kicked as hard as he could but the door didn't give in to the pressure. The tears streamed down his face as he pounded the door with his fists. Ted placed his foot against the wall and pulled as hard as he could. Through labored gasps he said, "Cliff, push!"

The two boys pushed and pulled with all their might and the door creaked and gave way, sending Ted tumbling into the metal shelving unit that housed the glass jars. The shelf came crashing down on top of Ted and smashed to pieces, sending pickled vegetables hurling across the floor. Cliff tumbled out of the fridge landing face first into pickle juice as the glass slashed his cheek and arms.

The two boys looked at each other with terror at what could have transpired if the door hadn't opened.

Cliff sat up, still looking at his brother. Blood began streaming down his arms and face from the now-throbbing wounds. Ted rubbed his head laughing. "Wow, that was close."

Their mother came barreling down the stairs to see what happened. The shock was apparent on her face, and the boys knew they would be grounded for a very long time.

Larry's voice brought Cliff back to the boardroom and away from the horrible scene in his head.

"Leave the boy alone. Maybe he can find something I missed. You never know." Larry smiled at Cliff. "I have been known to be wrong once in a while. I say, good thinking, lad."

Larry knew damn well why Cliff didn't want to go. Just the thought of going into the dense jungle didn't give him a good feeling either. Cliff, like many people, suffered from acute claustrophobia. Getting him in the dark jungle might just throw him into a panic attack or worse. He would be of no use to the team; it would be better off keeping him busy in the lab doing something constructive.

"Done! Larry, you and Randy see what you can find. I'll have the dean find a tracker to take you out. I don't want to have to come find you if you get lost," Marcus said with a broad grin. "Take what you need but keep it simple. You're going to have a bit of a hike, I gather."

Randy rolled his eyes. "Oh great, that's all I need. I get to smell Larry all the way there."

Larry gritted his teeth and glanced at Marcus. "Do I get permission to poison him while we are out if he gets out of hand?"

Marcus shook his head wondering if it was such a good idea teaming up these two.

Vanessa laughed aloud. "I don't know how we all lasted as a team for all these years."

With that, everyone except Vanessa got up and filed out of the room. A chill ran up her spine as if a cool breeze had suddenly struck her. She turned to scan the room and could have sworn someone was watching her. But that would be ridiculous; there wasn't anyone in the room but the team, and there were no windows either. She pulled her summer jacket close around her in the attempt to comfort her now-tingling skin.

She had heard about wackos putting tiny cameras in various places to watch people without their knowledge. The thought left her mind as quickly as it came. She was just paranoid; being back in Peru must be getting to her. Maybe it was the heat; she would have to take a cool shower when she got back to her room. Yeah, that was a good idea. Vanessa turned to leave the room unaware that on a bookshelf in the corner of the room, eight eyes sat watching her.

The vibrant creature took a step forward. The unseen visitor peered down at an obviously shaken Vanessa.

One long cobalt blue hairy leg stretched forward as if to beckon Vanessa, but she did not see it. She instead left the room and turned off the light leaving the mysterious creature to disappear into the darkness.

. . . .

A high-pitched buzzing of the alarm clock filled the air as the sun began to rise. As if by coincidence, parrots began to squawk in the distance, and Jim opened his eyes to the tropical melody outside.

It had been a late night from what he remembered, and his sudden headache reminded him of the few too many drinks he had consumed.

He reached to turn off the piercing ring of the alarm clock, and as he did so his hand brushed on something soft, a material of some kind. The feeling ran a cold chill down Jim's spine, and a piercing pain shot right through his temples.

He picked up the piece of material and examined the pair of women's satin underpants with lace around the trim and a slight scent of the woman who had worn them.

Flashes of moments from the night before suddenly raced through his mind in short confused bursts. He wasn't sure what he was seeing, but the memories disturbed him greatly. He saw a lady—not just any lady, a beautiful lady with raven black hair—flashes of Taylor Lemay holding her in his arms, the two of them dancing all night long.

The thought of a punk student having his way with such an esteemed woman angered him. He tried to remember what happened after the bar closed, but sudden flashes of light shot through Jim's head causing horrendous pain as if a lightning bolt struck right through his skull.

He refocused, shaking his head as he walked into the bathroom and turned on the shower. Hot streams of water jutted out onto the cool surface of the tub. Jim gazed at the constant flow for a moment mesmerized, imagining the water was the fingers of the nightingale from last night, calling him, beckoning him, wanting to touch him so badly.

Jim stepped into his cascading fantasy feeling the warmth of the water on his skin, caressing and teasing his senses.

He closed his eyes and ran his hand slowly down his chest until he got to his growing groin. He reached down and turned the water hotter so the jets of water could massage him and add to the fantasy.

Looking down he softly stroked his hardening shaft with a sense of longing. He placed his hand against the shower wall to steady himself as his head shot back and all of his senses went into overdrive.

The burning started in his scrotum and forced his stroking motion to increase as the orgasm came in long powerful erratic jolts. Losing control, his knees gave way, almost sending Jim crumbling to the hard tiled floor.

He gasped for air and tried to catch his breath, as every muscle was aching from the sheer strain. Jim kept his eyes closed so he could still enjoy the euphoria of pure ecstasy a little bit longer. Exhausted, he struggled to turn toward the streams of water to rinse the sweat off his face.

Jim couldn't remember the last time he had an orgasm like that. It certainly wasn't with manual labor, that was for damn sure. He couldn't even remember if he had gotten laid last night.

The warm water beat down on his chest, washing away the sweat and aroma of last night's drinking binge. He reached down to grab the soap with one hand and used the other to wipe his eyes. Suddenly he saw something out of the corner of his eye hanging from one of his fingers. His first thought was that it was the semen from his ejaculation, but this was different. It hung like thick threads of white … *cotton* …

He snapped his head down to look at his penis with a bewildered gaze. There, on his member, hung the white sticky cottonlike substance. Jim's breath caught in his throat. He slowly turned around and gazed at the shower walls to find strands upon strands of detailed webbing all over the tiles. A sudden strained scream escaped his body as he shook violently and collapsed to the porcelain floor below.

Almost all spiders have venom, but the purpose is to stun or kill their insect prey, not to harm humans. Only about twenty-five are thought to have venom that has an effect on humans. The two best known and feared venomous spiders are the black widow and the brown recluse. They have not been proven to have caused any deaths in more than two decades.

Chapter 6

Larry was excited to finally be going out to do some fieldwork, but most of all he wanted to get an up close and personal look at the country they were in. They had been stuck in the university for days, and it was getting a little old. They needed to break free for a while, get some fresh air, meet the locals, and not be so intimate with petri dishes.

Randy complained most of the morning about the lady friend he was leaving behind and that she could have been a good asset to have on the trip as a guide because she was a native to this country.

Larry looked at Randy in disgust. "Yeah right, I could just see it. The only thing she will be guiding is in your pants, or lack of what's in your pants, and we will never get anything done. Personally I think Vanessa should be coming with us. *She* is a good asset to have. She knows fieldwork better than you and me put together."

Randy scoffed. "Oh sure, you want *your* honey on the trip but not mine. Then we really wouldn't get anything done. You would be too busy looking at *her* assets."

Larry dropped his bag, stormed up to a laughing Randy, put one hand on his throat, and then pulled his other arm back. His fist took flight, connecting with Randy's jaw with a loud whack, and pulled back for another hit when Vanessa walked into the room. She yelped and ran over to grab Larry's arm.

"Larry, what in God's name do you think you are doing? Stop it! Get your hands off his throat! You're choking him!"

The sound of Vanessa's panic-stricken voice brought Larry back down to ground level, and he dropped his hands and then turned to look at her. Vanessa could see the rage in his eyes. He stepped back away from both of them, walked back to his bag, and snorted, "You're one lucky asshole. Next time I won't stop." He picked it up and hurried out of the room.

Randy coughed and sputtered for a moment and caught his breath. In labored gasps he grabbed Vanessa's arm. "Did you see that? He was going to kill me! I can't go out in the jungle with that maniac. I might not come back! I think he broke my jaw!"

Vanessa thought for a moment of the possibilities of that particular situation. Though the thought of Randy gone forever intrigued her, the logical side of her brain brought her back to reality.

"He wouldn't have killed you. He would have beaten you within an inch of your life though. I'm going to kick myself for a very long time for stopping him. I've wanted to do that for a long, long time." Pulling her arm out of Randy's grasp she continued. "And if you don't get you hands off me, I will!" The indifference in her voice made him feel a little uneasy.

Randy realized that he really wasn't liked much by his teammates. He watched her turn and walk out of the room as he rubbed his aching jaw. He suddenly wished he hadn't come to Peru. All the years he was on Marcus's team, he thought that they all just liked joking around as much as he did. It never occurred to him that they might really not like him. Randy had a sudden sense of emptiness. He picked up his bag and left the room too.

Vanessa ran down the hall to catch up with Larry, but he was long gone. She turned and walked toward the cafeteria instead to see if he was there. Suddenly she felt like she was being watched again and quickly turned around to see an agitated Jim Dunstan. His eyes as big as saucers, he looked like he hadn't slept in days. He was shaking like he had too much coffee and was white as a ghost.

When Vanessa turned toward him he acted like a scared child, dropping all the papers he had in his hands and suddenly looking disoriented. He lurched to the floor to retrieve the papers, and Vanessa rushed to his aid.

"Oh my god, Jim, are you all right? You look like shit. Do you want me to call Dr. Stein?" She reached over to check his forehead for a fever, but Jim cowered from her and hurried to pick up the documents before she could get a look at them. Jim didn't know what was happening to him, but he had to find out quickly. The experiment had been going on for months. He knew he was taking a risk, but he had to know what would happen. With Lydia gone he couldn't see how she was reacting to the experiment. How could he have lost her? How stupid! Lydia was his prize possession; she was going to make him rich and very well-known. She was going to change the arachnid world forever. They had to find her fast before all was lost.

"No … no, I am fine. I just have a deadline to marking these papers for my class. I was up all night doing it, and I'm not done yet. Thank you for your concern, Miss Thompson, but I must go now."

Vanessa watched in amazement as Jim ran down the hall like a scared animal. Was this really the man she met last night at the meeting who stood so tall and confident? His presence preceded him in the boardroom, and yet now he shrieked away from his own shadow. She could hardly believe her eyes.

Shaking her head she turned back toward the cafeteria and started talking to herself. "What the hell is going on here? It's like someone has injected people with a stupid drug." She opened the door to find that Larry wasn't in the cafeteria. There was no point running around after him. If he wanted to talk he would have to find her. She walked toward the lab to get back to her files.

In the corner down the hall, the eight-eyed predator lurked, watching the whole scene. For a moment Vanessa felt uneasiness come over her but then shrugged it off as paranoia once again.

She thought to herself, *It must be the climate. The heat is brutal, and I still haven't gotten a chance to go to the beach, if only to bask in the sun on a blow-up and feel the waves under my feet with the coolness on my toes.* The thought made her smile as she walked down the hall. She turned the corner as Marcus slammed right into her with such a force it knocked her to the ground.

"Oh shit! Vanessa, I'm sorry. Are you okay?" Marcus reached out his hand to help her up. Stunned and disoriented, Vanessa took his hand and stood up on wobbly legs.

"Jesus, Marc, I could have broken my tailbone. Where the hell's the fire?" Marcus tried to help Vanessa dust off her rear end, but to his disappointment she slapped his hand away. "I can do that myself, thank you!"

With a hurt look on his face, he began to explain his actions. "I was looking for you, actually."

Vanessa groaned. "Well you found me, but the next time you are looking, could you make it a little less painful please?" She rubbed her backside. "Make that a lot less painful."

Marcus suddenly felt sheepish. "I'm sorry but I've been looking through some files and need your opinion. That is, if you have the time." He put on the pouting face that Vanessa always hated. Through gritted teeth she took the offer, not because she wanted to help Marcus but because it was better than doing nothing at all in the lab.

They walked down to an empty office and sat down. Marcus poured them both a cup of coffee from the coffeemaker in the corner of the room and then sat down next to Vanessa. Marcus pulled the file out of his briefcase and handed it to Vanessa, who noticed the name on the file: jim dunstan, private and confidential.

"Uh, Marc, what are you doing with these?" Vanessa asked with a nervous tone. If they were caught with these personal files, nothing good could possibly come out of it.

Marcus grinned mischievously. "I have my ways around things, so don't you worry your pretty head. I know what you are thinking and nothing bad is going to happen."

Vanessa hated it when he could practically read her mind. It was such an intrusion of her privacy. "Well, I can think of a few things— disbandment, deportation, lawsuit—just to name a couple."

Marcus sat back in his chair. "For one thing, you can't be disbanded because I am your boss, so relax. The dean knows I have them."

Vanessa looked at him with shock. "Another word, among many, just popped in my head, like *accomplice*!"

Marcus let out a hearty laugh. "I don't think so. He just happened to conveniently but accidentally leave the door to the office open."

Vanessa glared at him in shock. "Okay, so what do you need them for?" Tapping her foot nervously, she put the file on her lap and flipped through it cautiously.

"Well, I didn't have a good feeling about our buddy Jim from the moment I met him. Then I found out he was performing the autopsies of the tribesmen they brought in. I still don't know if he was alone, but what he put in the files didn't seem to match up with what I was seeing and hearing from the dean and others who have been on the case. That is why I wanted you here with me. I figured the boys could handle everything in the field without you."

Now it was Vanessa's turn to laugh. "You wouldn't have said that a while ago if you witnessed what I did in the lab." Marcus had a questioning look, and Vanessa figured she should tell him the truth before Larry and Randy left, so she proceeded to tell him the story. A few moments later she added, "So you see I don't know if you really want them to go alone."

Marcus grinned. "Well, they will either learn to like each other or they will kill each other, and as far as I am concerned neither is a bad thing."

Vanessa leaned over and smacked his arm. "You are such an asshole at times." She giggled. "So what is the latest newsbreak on these files?"

Marcus bent forward to flip the pages in the front of the file, which happened to still be on Vanessa's lap. "I went to dig up Jim's name on the police archives and, look, a few years ago Dr. Dunstan had a criminal record. I don't think anyone but the dean knows about it either. Then I found out that the dean owed the mayor a favor. You see, Jim is the mayor's son, and it seems that old Jimmy boy couldn't get a job after all that, so the dean leant a hand. However, before he was thrown in the slammer, Jim worked for some very famous and credible companies. That wasn't a great way to end his career." Marcus paused.

Vanessa frowned. "Back up a minute. Number one, how the hell did you get into the police archives? And two, what has that got to do with the reason we are here? So the guy got a break. No crime in that."

Marcus flipped the page. "To answer number one, I still have some connections around here. Leave it at that. To answer number two, take a look." He pointed at the line in the file that told the crime committed.

Vanessa let out a gasp and put her hand to her mouth. "Oh my god, he raped a woman? Okay … okay, so that still doesn't tie into why we are here."

"No, it doesn't, but I still think he is bad news. Something in my gut is telling me he is somehow involved." Marcus bit his lip.

"So now you're going to accuse him of murder too? Marc, I think you are going a little off track with this. One has nothing to do with the other." Closing the file she handed it back to Marcus.

"Maybe not, but I do want you to stick close, okay? I just don't trust the guy. Promise you won't leave the campus, Kitty. I couldn't handle it if—" He caught the words in his throat.

Vanessa hadn't heard him call her "Kitty" in years, and suddenly she knew he was seriously worried about her safety. She leaned over and put a hand on his. "Okay, baby, I promise."

Marcus looked into her eyes and for a brief moment was taken by surprise. He longed for her tender caresses. They just stared at each other, and nothing else was said.

Spiders can't chew or swallow, so they inject their prey with poison. The poison turns the insides of insects to a watery substance so the spider can drink it.

Chapter 7

Shyla felt her heartbeat in her head pounding louder and louder as the minutes passed. Her body felt numb and she couldn't see anything but a blur. Her womanhood ached with a pain she had never felt before that made her wince. She felt like she had been drugged, her head was spinning like a top, and her thoughts were scattered. She tried to talk but her mouth was dry, causing the words to catch in her throat. A sudden fear came over her. *Where am I? What happened? How did I get here?*

Shyla could hear something in the distance but couldn't quite make it out. It was similar to a ticking sound, or was it a scratching sound? It wasn't clear enough to be certain. She tried to move, but her hands were bound with something heavy, like metal shackles. Panic struck as the reality of her situation came into focus: she had been tied up. She began to fight against the restraints, but they cut into her skin. Shyla's whole body was restrained, not just her hands and legs, and her legs were spread apart in a most vulnerable position. As her vision started to return, she tried hard to focus on one thing at a time, looking around at the walls, the ceiling, the floor, and the door.

Wait a minute! The floor? What the hell! If I'm lying down, I wouldn't be able to see the floor. I'd be lying on something, like a bed or a table.

She glanced from side to side at her hands, then down at her feet, and then her body. She was naked and spread eagle. She noticed mud on her feet and bruises on her arms. A pain shot through her, and she came to a terrifying conclusion that she had been raped and beaten.

Her eyes darted madly around the room, her head lolling from side to side in her drug-induced fog, realizing that she was attached to the wall as if she were a painting on display for all to see. How long had she been here? Shyla couldn't be sure, but it couldn't have been that long. She shivered from the cold wall at her back.

She heard a door open and then close loudly. It sounded like a bay door to a garage. Horror gripped her at the thought of her abductor coming back to torment her. Shyla tried again to fight against the restraints but stopped when she heard a voice.

"There's no point, sweetheart, you're just wasting your energy." She couldn't see him yet, but she sure knew the voice. It was the guy from the bar. What was his name? There was no mistaking that smooth masculine voice.

She cleared her sore, scratchy throat and tried again to speak. "What are you doing? Why are you doing this to me? Please let me go. I promise I won't tell anyone who you are." As soon as she said it, she wished she hadn't. It sounded so ridiculous. All victims say the same thing, and they damn well know they will tell if given the chance.

He came around the corner so she could see whom it was coming up real close and running his fingers down her cheek. "Of course you won't tell anyone, my sweet. I trust you fully. I will let you go as soon as I am finished with you, but we haven't had nearly enough fun yet."

His fingers ran farther down her body as he talked and stopped at her nipple. He gave it an unforgiving squeeze, and Shyla screamed in pain.

"Yeah, baby, that's right. Let it out. No one can hear you anyway. Come on, baby, scream!"

Shyla closed her mouth, realizing he was getting aroused from hearing her suffering. His hard member stretched his pants to their limit, and Shyla's stomach turned at the sight. He squeezed her nipple harder, and she let out an agonizing moan, biting her lip so hard it tore the skin. "Come on, baby, don't you want to scream for me?"

She closed her eyes and tried to think of something else so as not to encourage him with her misery.

"Oh, okay, you're going to play it the hard way. That's fine. I can play that game too." He ran his fingers even farther down to reach the raw, aching, mound between her legs. Shyla's eyes shot open with terror. Her voice screamed in her mind, *Oh god no, not again! I can't take anymore. I have to get out … but how?* She glared straight into his eyes and spat in his face.

"You bastard! I'll kill you when I get loose." Then her tone changed, becoming a little more defiant. She wasn't sure if it was a good idea, but she had heard of women who verbally attacked their abductors and the men usually backed down. *Don't allow them to see that you are afraid.*

"You're a sick fucker, aren't you? I bet your mama and daddy fucked you once or twice when you were a child! That's probably why you feel the need to abuse women, don't you? You need to feel like a man because you're—" The slap came across her face before she could get the sentence out and left her ears ringing.

"You fuckin' little bitch! You think I am some pathetic little man, don't you? You think I am some psycho case straight from the mental ward. Man, have you got it wrong!" He raised his hand again and brought it down across her face once more. Blood trickled down her cheek from the slice in her skin cause from the ring on his finger. The broken blood vessels in her eye filled her vision with a red haze.

At that moment, Shyla knew she wasn't dealing with a loony case and that he was going to kill her.

. . . .

As they drove down the bumpy dirt road into the immenseness of the jungle, Larry began to see the absolute beauty of the landscape that he had failed to notice when they came to the university the week before.

He took a deep breath, taking in the sweet smells of the land. The air was rich with the intensely dense smell of the rain forest. He began to remember a time when he was a little boy and his family traveled to many places around the world, including Thailand, Egypt, and Spain.

His favorite, however, was Taman Negara National Park in Malaysia, where one of the plants, the Zingiber, would twist and strangle every tree trunk in its path with leaves cascading down the branches encasing them in a shroud of mystery. The stem displays clusters of tightly closed bright orange spindle-shaped stocks with flowers pushing their way out.

The daydream came to an abrupt end as the Jeep hit a considerable bump in the road, stopping them dead in their tracks.

Larry smacked his head on the roll bar right above him. Randy was rudely awakened as his body bounced and was thrown forward against the seats in front of him. Getting his bearings, he began yelling at the guide.

"What the hell! Don't you know how to drive?" Randy looked angrily at Larry. "I can't believe Marcus is paying this idiot to drive us out. We will be lucky to get there in one piece if this keeps up!" Randy scolded as he clumsily got back in his seat.

Larry rubbed the bump forming on his head, shot a glance at Randy, and then grumbled under his breath, "Not if I get you first, you little prick!"

Larry stuck his head out the door to look at the front tire to see what the damage was. They were caught up on a boulder that was now wedged under the axle.

The driver stepped out of the Jeep, looked underneath the chassis, and started cursing. "Piece of shit!"

Larry and Randy looked at each other as they started to get out of the vehicle. Larry grinned. "Well, that's the first thing I have understood come out of his mouth all day. I guess that means the ride stops here and we walk."

Grabbing as much gear as they could handle, the three men began the journey into the jungle by foot. There was only a few hours of daylight left, and they wanted to find a place to camp for the night and continue the rest of the way in the morning. The dense damp jungle and crisp air were a refreshing change from the city. The sound of parrots and peacocks echoed and bounced off the trees, and the sunbeams became scattered as they walked along the weather-beaten path. The moss squished beneath their shoes, making the men unsure of their footing.

Randy had visions of quicksand engulfing his body as Larry watched him sink into the earth without a trace, laughing and clapping as the sand engulfed him. He shuddered at the thought and quickly pushed it out of his head.

Larry, on the other hand, was quite enjoying his surroundings. As he looked around he spotted different animals all over the jungle. A monkey swung in the tree above them, and a snake slithered across the makeshift trail they walked down. He never told Randy about the snake; otherwise he would have had to pick Randy up off the ground and carry him on his back the rest of the way, and he really didn't feel like doing that.

The sun began its descent, and coolness touched the air. The guide stopped to look around and then took a turn to the right.

Randy raised his eyebrow. "And what does he think he is doing?"

Larry shrugged his shoulders and followed the man. They stopped in an open clearing that was less than comforting, as it was also open to all the elements that Mother Nature could throw in their direction.

The guide dropped his packs and the rest of his gear, turned, and muttered in his native tongue, "La selva es peligroso."

Larry wasn't at all sure what he was saying, and Randy was desperately looking through his multilingual dictionary in hopes of catching just one word. The guide started pointing to the forest and making a motion. "No go."

Larry glanced at Randy "Well, I think a monkey could figure out that there is something fishy here." He turned and looked at the trees. Randy snickered and, without looking up from his book, said, "Isn't that your deodorant?"

Larry just ignored the comment, knowing it wasn't worth his time to retort. Suddenly they heard a ghastly high-pitched screech of an animal. Stopping in their tracks, they glared at the guide. Randy grabbed him by the shirt and shook him. "What the hell have you gotten us into?"

Larry tried to get Randy to release the man to no avail. Randy's terror had taken over with an adrenaline rush that gave him a charge of strength. The guide recoiled and tried to break Randy's grip.

Larry just let them struggle, watching in amusement and looking through the little book Randy had brought.

The guide was saying particular words over and over—*muerte* and *peligro*—so Larry began to look for that word, not having a clue how to spell it but giving it a try anyway. After a moment he found some words that looked close and read them under his breath: "Danger, death ... *oh, shit!* Randy!"

Larry dropped the book, grabbed Randy by the shoulder, and swung him around to face him. "Randy, shut the fuck up for a minute!"

Randy looked at Larry in astonishment. Hearing profanity come out of Larry's mouth made him drop the guide. In the whole time he knew this man, the only other time he heard him swear like that was when his ex-wife hit him up for everything he owned.

"What? Calm down, Larry. Breathe, for Christ's sake!"

Larry took a deep breath, "The guide is trying to tell us that there is some kind of danger in the jungle up ahead! We must be real close to the Quichua village. He wants us to sleep out here so we will be out in the open and can see anything that comes our way. It would be easily spotted out here." He looked toward the jungle. "This must be where the villagers were found."

Randy's face went completely white, and he began to shake uncontrollably. He slowly turned toward the forest, the reality of what they heard a few moments ago sinking in. "You don't think … it might have been a human, do you?"

Larry looked at Randy with astonishment. "No, you idiot. For all we know it could have been a mating ritual. At any rate I think we should go check it out and see if we can get to the village."

"Are you nuts? I vote to wait until morning. It's already getting dark." Randy shuttered.

Larry looked up at the sky. "Okay, but we start out first thing in the morning."

Reluctantly Randy agreed. For the next two hours they began to make camp.

Believe it or not a Daddy Long Legs is not a spider. They are a different class called harvestmen. They have three body sections, and their legs have seven sections. Their legs can break off to surprise or distract their predators.

Chapter 8

Jim sat in the lab looking over the file folders of paperwork on the experiment he had been working on, charts, and toxicology results. He wasn't sure what he was looking for; maybe one of the base pairs was in the wrong sequence. He could make a couple changes to the DNA sequencing and hope for the best. Suddenly, he heard a key enter the lock to the lab room Jim was in. Quickly, he fumbled with the files and put the vials back in the fridge to keep cool.

Cliff entered the room, and Jim nervously sat back down. "Oh, hi there, Cliff." Cliff looked up with a start. "Jesus! Oh, man, you scared the hell out of me. I thought I was the only one here."

Jim chuckled. "You're not the only one who works late. I'm just finishing up on some paperwork. I'll be out of your way in a second."

Cliff made a hand gesture. "Oh, don't worry about it. I am just coming to put back these samples. Then I'm off to bed." Cliff opened the fridge door and put down the tray he was holding. Jim drew a quick breath, hoping Cliff didn't notice anything unusual.

Cliff closed the door and turned back to Jim. "Well, I'm off to dreamland." Turning slightly he noticed the syringe on the counter that had rolled behind a lab flask. "Oh, man, someone needs to be more careful." He pointed to the needle. "You better get that in a sharps container and talk to your students about that."

Jim picked up the needle and laughed. "Yeah, you're right. Thanks. I guess I haven't taught them everything now, have I?"

Cliff smiled and walked away, closing the door behind him. Jim slouched on the stool scratching his head. *Wow, that was close.* He closed the files and placed them in his briefcase. Then he picked up his belongings, shut off the light, and walked out of the lab.

· · · · · · · · · · · · · ·

Vanessa rubbed her eyes and stretched her back. It had been a long night at the lab and not too enlightening. Her focus kept coming back to the conversation that she and Marcus had that afternoon, and she found it too hard to concentrate on anything else.

She decided to go grab a drink somewhere to help her relax before going to bed. She had remembered a bar outside of town that was a pretty good place to go. Packing up her belongings and grabbing her jacket, she headed out of the lab.

There were some students still up working on papers in the library and in labs. She was taken back to when she was in this same university, staying up till all hours of the night working on stuff for class the next day that should have been finished days before. That was what happened when frat parties got in the way. She chuckled to herself remembering the hangovers that came along with them. As she walked down the hall toward the main part of the building, she noticed the janitor cleaning the floors in the halls.

The woman looked up and smiled gingerly. She had her hair in a neat bun. Her skin was an olive tone, and her cheekbones protruded like that of a porcelain doll. Vanessa had an idea and smiled back, walking toward the lady pretending to look somewhat urgent. The lady, seeing the look on Vanessa's face, frowned. "My dear, what is the matter?"

Vanessa noticed the ring of keys hanging from the woman's belt. She put her hands on her hips, turned her gaze down the hall, and pointed.

"I am so glad I found you. I did something really stupid. You see, my office is down the hall here and I locked my keys in there. I tell you, sometimes I could just kick myself for the dumb things I do. Could you help me?"

The women walked down the hall together. Vanessa continued. "I am new here, and I'm not used to those damn self-locking doors." Then she giggled. "I feel a little foolish really."

The janitor looked at Vanessa and gave her a gesture. "Ah, don't worry your pretty head about it, sweetie. We all do it. I remember a time when I locked my whole key ring in an office once." Lifting the ring, she jiggled it. "What a fiasco that was. I had to call my boss at four in the morning and get him out of bed to open the door for me. I really thought I lost my job for that one." The women laughed.

"Which one is it, dear?" Vanessa looked at the names on the doors in a way so that the woman wouldn't think she forgot where her office was as well.

She pointed to a door. "Here it is." The woman looked at the name on the plate: "Prof. J. Dunstan, Head of Entomology and Biology." Then she gave a surprised look, and Vanessa thought she was busted.

She never stopped to think that the woman might know Jim Dunstan. She held her breath, not sure what to do next.

The lady chuckled. "Well, my goodness, you have your own department to yourself." She snorted. "It's no wonder you don't have your head about your shoulders. You are a very busy girl!"

Vanessa exhaled and then looked around to make sure no one was watching. She leaned over to whisper in the woman's ear. "Don't let anyone else hear you say that. I am supposed to be like Joan of Arc. Strong, tough, I can handle anything. If it gets out to my students that I am just human and make mistakes … I am doomed."

The woman let out a laugh that warmed Vanessa's soul. "Your secret is safe with me, dear." She opened the door and then bid Vanessa a good night. "If there is anything else you need, you know where to find me."

Vanessa thanked her, took another quick look around, and closed the door behind her. She wasn't at all sure what she was doing or what she was looking for, but she knew she had to look anyway. She turned on the small desk light hoping it wouldn't give off too much light. She had to work fast before anyone caught her. When her eyes adjusted to the dim lighting, she spotted a filing cabinet, quickly walked over, and tried to open it, but it was locked. She glanced at the desk and found what she was looking for. There was a bowl of paper clips, and she began to unbend one, thinking to herself, *Well, I guess the old boyfriends came in handy after all.* She remembered all the things they taught her, no matter how meager, one of which was lock picking.

She inserted the clip into the keyhole and wiggled it around until she felt a soft piece, like a sponge, and pushed on it. It gave way and the cabinet opened. She placed the clip between her teeth and started flipping through the files. They all looked like regular school files on his students, with letter grades on the project they had done during the year.

Vanessa was about to give up on that drawer when she spotted a file way at the back that looked a little different than the rest. All it had was the name "Lydia" and a bar code of some sort. Peaking Vanessa's interest, she pulled it out, placed it on the desk, and flipped it open.

Most of the papers were newspaper clippings started from twenty years prior. Vanessa didn't think much of it until her eyes caught a headline: Twenty-one-year-old woman found raped and beaten to death in a staten island park.

She read the first paragraph in shocked disbelief.

On Wednesday morning twenty-one-year-old Tina Peterson's body was found in Wolfe's Pond Beach Park by a local resident jogging in the area. Her body lay naked and battered under a bush. Authorities say she was a victim of a horrific rape. They are cautioning everyone to stay in their homes and to stay away from the park ...

Vanessa looked at the picture of the girl. She was wearing her graduation cap and gown, holding a bouquet of red roses. Vanessa also realized that she was possibly looking at one of Jim Dustan's victims. She flipped through more pages and found more victims from all over the globe.

GIRL DIES BY ASPHYXIATION IN OKARITO LAGOON
Mostala Balamore, a fourteen-year-old New Zealand resident was discovered by Parks and Recreational Services last night after a call came in to police, saying that the girl had not made it home from school ...

Vanessa put her hand to her mouth not believing what she was reading. She again looked at the picture at the top left corner of the page. The girl looked much younger than her age. The thought of a child being penetrated by a fully grown man made her nauseous. She read on:

... The girl was raped, beaten, and suffocated then left for dead.

Lydia

Vanessa kept flipping the pages unable to take her eyes off the ghastly stories.

SALTSPRING SHOCKED BY BRUTAL MURDER OF LOCALS
Laria Greensmithe and husband John Greensmithe were found dead on their twenty-foot boat between Pender and Salt Spring Islands Friday after a brutal attack from, who friends believe, was a man that the couple had met that day at a local pub. The couple asked the man to come out fishing with them, unaware of their fate. Laria, twenty-eight years old, was tied up, raped, and then bludgeoned to death. John, forty, was viciously stabbed fifteen times in the chest and tied to the bow of the vessel, where he bled to death ...

Vanessa's breath caught in her throat as the tears streamed down her face. The sickening acts of violence played like a movie in Vanessa's head. It was a movie that couldn't be turned off. She closed the file with shaking hands and steadied herself. As she turned, the wave of nausea hit again as dizziness overcame her, and Vanessa grabbed the filing cabinet to get her balance. Trying to place the folder in the drawer, a couple of the pages fell to the floor. Bending down to pick them up, Vanessa tried to focus on them to get them back in the sheath. The larger-than-life headline stood out: missing local woman could be the next on serial killer's list.

Vanessa walked over to the photocopier and began scanning as many pages as she possibly could. After she was finished she returned the folder to the cabinet and then picked up the phone. She had to tell Marcus what she found. She tapped her fingers on the desk impatiently.

"Dr. Tolson speaking."

"Marc, it's Vanessa. We have to talk." Little did Vanessa know Jim Dustan was listening from the hallway just outside the door.

. . . .

Shyla awoke to the sound of someone rustling around in the room adjacent to her. He was out of her line of view so she couldn't tell what he was doing. He gathered the supplies that he needed and carefully placed them on a cart.

God knew the supplies cost a fortune, but eventually it would all pay off, tripling his money. He would have no problems attracting investors from large corporations. They would be pounding down his door to buy the rights—not that they were for sale, but the thought was nice.

He wheeled the supplies into the next room and locked the padlock behind him. He looked up to find a distressed Shyla looking back.

"Good morning, sunshine. I hope you slept well. You have a big day ahead of you." He tried to sound as jovial as he could, but it didn't help the situation.

"You sick asshole! What have you got to be so happy about? Oh wait, I know. Let's see. You have a woman tied up and at your disposal at any fuckin' moment your perverted little pea brain wants to use her." Shyla took a breath long enough to gaze at the items on the cart. She wasn't sure what everything was, but she recognized some things. Plastic intravenous tubing, needles, pumps, gauges, cotton swabs, and various other items were situated before her.

Shyla spat the words out so fast it surprised even her. "What the hell do you think you are going to do with all that?"

He grinned. "Like I said, you have a big day ahead of you."

Shyla's fear gripped her like a vice, and it showed on her face. He snickered and began. "Oh, please. You can't tell me that you thought you were just here for my sexual pleasure, did you?" Shyla nodded sorrowfully, and his laugh penetrated the very core of her being.

"Well, it just wouldn't be all that exciting, now, would it? No, I have plans for you, my sweet." He caressed her cheek with the palm of his hand and marveled at the softness. He felt a twitch in his pants as his member responded. He brushed it across Shyla's legs and gleamed.

"Oh, now look what you've gone and done. You see, you bring it all on yourself, cupcake." He turned and picked up the syringe. "I am going to take a blood sample now. It won't hurt a bit if you stay still. I wouldn't want to break the needle off in your arm."

Shyla stayed as still as she could muster. He swabbed her arm with alcohol and then inserted the needle. She stiffened as the pain shot up her bicep. "What the hell did you use, a horse needle?"

He chuckled. "Sorry, I couldn't get ahold of any girly needles. All I could manage was an eighteen-gauge needle. It is big enough to get the job done." He turned and walked away. "I will be right back. Don't go anywhere, okay?"

Shyla spat on the ground in disgust. Her thoughts came in waves, and she had difficulty keeping track. The question most forefront in her mind was what his intentions were. She didn't want to ponder that very long because no matter what it was she knew it wasn't going to be good.

She suddenly felt her stomach growling. *Man, how long have I been here?* It had to be at least a week. She wasn't quite sure. Shyla looked down at her pubic area and frowned. Her attacker had shaved her completely, and a catheter was inserted so she could urinate. Plus a bag was taped to her with duct tape so she had somewhere to defecate.

How kind, she thought in distaste. A small part of her was thankful that she didn't have to sit in a room smelling of human waste. She smiled at the reminder that the captor had to change the bag. She was determined to deposit a big bowel movement in the bag and watch him remove it, hopefully causing him to retch. The vision disappeared as he walked back in the room.

"Well, we are all ready to go, the stage is set, and it is *showtime*!" He picked up a brown bottle, poured some chloroform on a white cloth, and turned toward Shyla. "Good night, my dear. I will see you soon." He placed the cloth over Shyla's mouth and nose. Her body shuddered against him. Her vision started to blur and her mouth became dry. Then the room went dark.

There are approximately 111 spider families and around forty thousand spider species in the world, but there might be as many as two hundred thousand different species in total.

Chapter 9

Marcus sat in his room, savoring the quiet that came over the dorm, and picked up the local newspaper. He was tired of looking at files and charts, and he decided that new material was a good change of pace.

Yawning, he unfolded the paper to see the bold headline along with a picture of a beautiful woman with long black hair. The caption read: missing local woman could be the next on serial killer's list.

Shyla Demone was last seen Tuesday at the Chiclaya Tavern. It is believed that she is the latest victim in the Peru serial killings.

Marcus put the paper down on his lap and thought for a moment. *Did the press already hear about the deaths? And now they think it's a serial killer.* "Damn! Someone must have leaked the news." He looked at the date on the paper. He raised his eyebrow and drew a slow breath. This paper was printed a couple days after the team had already arrived in Peru.

There was a sudden knock at the door, and Marcus rose to answer it. A very confused Cliff stood there looking at him. "Hey, Cliff. What's up? Come in and take a load off."

Cliff entered the small dorm room, found a seat on the bed, and handed the folder he was holding to his superior. "I'm sorry, Marcus. I know it's late, but I just didn't know what to do with this. I couldn't sleep so I went back to the lab." Marcus took the folder and opened it.

Cliff continued. "I was studying the samples I had, and I think I accidentally grabbed someone else's vial. Marcus, someone is doing some major experiments with DNA."

Suddenly the phone rang, and Marcus picked it up. He looked at Cliff and then put his hand over the receiver.

"It's Vanessa."

Cliff looked at his watch, thinking to himself, *What is Vanessa doing phoning at 11:00 pm?*

Marcus finished the short conversation and then put the receiver down. "Come on, Cliff, we have to go." He bent down to put on his shoes, grabbed his briefcase, and started for the door.

Cliff looked confused and said, "Marcus, what's up? Where are we going?"

Marcus stopped to check to see if he had his wallet and then looked back at Cliff. "Vanessa says she found something that we need to see. We're going to meet her at a club outside of town. You can tell me about your finding on the way." Cliff grabbed his papers and followed Marcus down the corridor.

. . . .

Vanessa hated driving in the dark, especially when she didn't know where she was going. When she turned on the radio to see what she could find, there was a soft melody of chimes and flutes. Granted, the words were all in Peruvian, but it was nice to listen to the music. She needed something to get her mind off her thoughts.

The landscape was very dark and there weren't any streetlights to guide her, like in the city. The cool air from the open window blew her hair away from her face. The air was welcomed as Vanessa began to relax and enjoy the ride. The sweet smell of the tropical flowers filled her nostrils, and her mind began to drift.

She thought about the trip she and Marcus had taken to Hawaii when they were dating. They stood on the rocky cliffs of Maui looking at the waterfall as it poured into the natural springs below. The beautiful valley of greenery went as far as the eyes could see, and the smells were tantalizing. That was the week Marcus told her he loved her. Not long after that, the relationship came to an end.

Vanessa realized that twenty minutes had passed and she wasn't even watching where she was going. She hoped she hadn't passed the turnoff. Squinting in the darkness she slowed the Jeep down. In the distance she saw a building that looked like a very broken-down warehouse. It seemed that no one had been in it for years. Vanessa tried to focus on the sign that was on the side road. It read: jd holdings inc. The rest of the sign was hanging by a hinge. It read in Spanish: keep out. tresspassers will be severely punished!

Vanessa decided to keep going on the road she was headed down. She hadn't seen any signs or lights to tell her where she was, but she had a feeling she was going the right way. Ten minutes later the road gave way to a sea of lights. On the side of the road a green sign said: chiclaya 1 mile.

Vanessa smiled. *See, a woman doesn't need a man to find her way. A drink is definitely in order.*

Jim Dunstan didn't need his headlights to guide him to Chiclaya. He could take this trip with his eyes closed. It helped to camouflage him too. He grinned. Vanessa had no idea he was right behind her. Getting in his business could be the worst and last thing she could have ever done. No one crossed Jim Dunstan, not even the pretty face of Vanessa Thompson.

. . . .

A shaken Randy helped their guide set up the four-man tent that was packed in the Jeep, and then he put all the equipment and supplies inside to keep them safe, away from animals and the elements. There were visions of cannibals in his mind as he looked off into the distance to the dark jungle.

Larry got the campfire ready for the night as the guide sat in a cross-legged position praying to his god for the hundredth time.

Randy looked at Larry, still white as a ghost. "Do you think it could have been cannibals? I mean, do they live here? Do you think they will come after us? Do you think—"

"Shut the hell up, Randy! If you say one more word I will personally send a message to them to come take you off my hands!" Larry's patience was running dangerously low.

He knew they would have to investigate it in the morning, but he wasn't sure if he was ready to handle what there was to see. A deathly quiet came over the jungle, and there was a chill in the air. Stoking the fire, Larry sat looking out into the darkness and strained to hear any remote sound of life. There was nothing, and he wondered if it always sounded this way or if it was caused by the unseen predators that lurked in the shadows beyond. Larry didn't want to think about what could be the cause of what they heard earlier.

The shadows wrapped around them like a black hole striving to engulf their vulnerable souls. The fire was burning bright and the flames licked the air in a desperate plea for more oxygen to keep it alive. Larry sat listening to the snapping and crackling, trying to think of other things. Picking up his notebook he began flipping through what he had written over the last few days. He began to narrow down different species of spiders in terms of location, qualities, and arachnid behavior. He began to read his own notes and pictures.

Arachnid name: Pamphobeteus
Translation: Violet Black Tarantula
This large tarantula is mainly found in South America in the depths of the rain forest. This spider does not use webbing and feeds on small reptiles. The carapace and legs of the females are a velvet-type texture with the color of blue-black. The abdomen is a sheen palette of long black hair with light brown on the rear half. The male is similar but the jaws, palpus, and legs are violet. Females can be seen all year long, but the males are uncertain.
Size: Female up to 60 mm, male up to 50 mm
Location: Peru and Bolivia (Amazonian)

Arachnid Name: Avicularia
Translation: Pink-toed Tarantula
This tarantula is well-known for its pink toes and wide range. The carapace and abdomen is covered in a coat of long black hair. You can find these beauties in amongst a pineapple plant and also folded banana leaves to build their silky nest. The pink toe mainly feeds on tree frogs and insects, but once in a while it may treat itself to a tasty roosting bird.
Size: Female up to 50 mm, male up to 35 mm
Location: Guyana, Brazil, Venezuela, and Trinidad

Larry looked up from his book for a moment to find Randy

struggling to get into his sleeping bag. The guide was sound asleep sitting upright in his prayer position snoring. Larry chuckled and went back to his reading.

Arachnid Name: Theraphosa Blondi
Translation: Goliath Tarantula
This is the largest spider in the world and has enough strength to overpower frogs, toads, lizards, mice, and small snakes. Their habitat is in the deep burrows in the rain forest. The male's leg span alone reaches 25 cm. When it rubs parts of its body together there is a clear audible sound.
Size: Female up to 90 mm, male up to 85 mm
Location: Venezuela, North Brazil, French Guiana, and Suriname

As if on cue like a finely turned play, Larry began to hear the eerie sounds of the night. In the not-so-far-off distance there was a nattering sound and a spine tingling hum that seemed to come from something much larger than a common cricket. Drums began to perform an rhythmic sequence of patterns that Larry knew was coming from a nearby tribe, a celebration of some kind of guest.

Putting his book down beside his sleeping bag, Larry snuggled down as if to seek comfort in what lay beyond the shadows.

To his left Randy was purring like a kitten. Larry let out a disgusted grunt assuming that Randy was dreaming about his many suitors, concubines, and whores. Randy was the one who was freaking out earlier and was now sleeping like a baby, and Larry was the one who couldn't sleep. The drums played louder and Larry's intrigue pumped through his veins with every beat.

The decision was made. He unzipped his sleeping bag and grabbed his jacket. He shook Randy out of his deep slumber and then began to pack a bag.

Randy grumbled and groaned and sat up. "What the hell are you doing?"

Larry clicked a flashlight on and off to make sure it worked, found some extra batteries, and then placed them in the bag. "Come on, get up. We are going to see where those drums are coming from. It will be easier at night. We won't be detected that way."

Randy looked astonished. "Please tell me you are joking, Larry, for gods sake! You have gone completely loco. We don't know what is out there. There could be wild animals or traps."

"Yeah, and we will be fine. The drumming doesn't sound like it's too far away from here, so come on." Larry finished putting the bag together and then stood looking at Randy impatiently. The guide stirred and rolled over.

Randy stood up and kicked his blanket. "So what, you want to go to a powwow? Man, you need to get out more, Larry. You need some friends."

The men started walking toward the forest with flashlights in hand unaware of the visitor walking ten feet to their left.

Its legs moved swiftly and quietly through the grass, the moonlight glistening on the soft cobalt blue hair that descended down the length of the four-and-a-half-inch legs. Moving swiftly around the tent, the predator scanned the area not sure what she was looking for. Then suddenly as if guided by radar, she found her target. Moving as fast as her legs could carry her immense frame, she closed in on her prey. She crawled around her victim once to find the crucial spot to strike.

Suddenly the victim opened his eyes and, before a scream could escape from his shaking lips, she sunk her fangs deep into his flesh flushing his body with deadly venom. His body convulsed and flinched with pain, the venom working its magic though his throbbing veins. As quickly as it started, it ended in total paralysis. Then … death. His eyes were still open as if beckoning the moon, like a final plea for help.

In the South Pacific, native people have made fishing nets from a spider's silk. People encourage Nephila spiders to build webs between two bamboo shoots, which are then used for angling.

Chapter 10

$\mathcal{M}$arcus ordered another round for him and Cliff and then looked at his watch. As if reading Marcus's mind, Cliff looked toward the door. "She should have been here by now."

Marcus got up from his seat. "I'm going to see if I can get ahold of her." He walked over to the telephones that sat in the corner of the bar room. He picked up the receiver and started to dial. Gazing out the window to his left he noticed someone walking toward the front door. He dropped the receiver back in its cradle. *She probably just got lost, but she is here now,* he thought. Marcus began walking toward the door when it flung open and Jim Dunstan walked in. Marcus stopped in his tracks. Jim turned to look at him and waved.

"Hey, Marcus, fancy meeting you here." Jim held out his hand and Marcus reluctantly took it.

"Hi, Jim, what brings you down here?" Marcus let go of Jim's hands, fighting the urge to wipe his hands on his pants in the attempt to get rid of the bad vibes.

Jim looked around and saw Cliff sitting at a table in the corner. "Oh, I just wanted to have a nightcap. It's been one of those days, you know."

Marcus scanned the room. "Are you meeting someone?"

"Uh … no, I just wanted to see if there was anyone I knew here tonight."

He stopped scanning to look at Marcus, who made an effort to smile, put a hand over his heart, and then made a gasping noise. "Oh, I'm hurt. What, we're not good enough for you?"

Jim rolled his eyes. "Oh, man, I'm sorry. I didn't mean that the way it sounded. Forgive me. May I sit with you guys?"

Marcus felt a shiver go through his body and fought to keep the words that were in his head from coming out of his mouth. He forced a pleasant gesture and slapped Jim's shoulder. "Oh, but of course. We are all on the same team." Marcus glared at Jim, creating a subtle challenge. "Right?"

Jim shot Marcus a quizzical look and thought, *What did he mean by that?*

As they walked over to the table Marcus shot a fretful look at Cliff, and Cliff moved over in the booth to make room for their new guest, not querying Marcus. Cliff knew all too well that there had to be a damn good reason for Marcus to bring the man they have been questioning over to sit with them.

Jim sat down and motioned to the bartender to give him his usual. Marcus motioned for another round for him and Cliff and then turned to face Jim. Jim glanced around the bar once more. "Is Vanessa here too?" Cliff opened his mouth to say something, and Marcus gave him a quick fierce look and then shook his head. Cliff shut his mouth again.

"No, as a matter of fact, she was pretty tired today. I guess the heat was getting to her so she decided to bail on us and hit the hay." Marcus frowned at his own play on words. "Man, that was bad."

Jim chuckled. "I've said worse."

The bartender cut in to put the drinks on the table and wink at Marcus. "Believe me, he has. Jim has a very appalling sense of humor. He was probably bored as a kid and had nothing better to do than come up with the worst jokes imaginable; either that or he was dropped on his head." He smiled again. "Or both."

Jim frowned at him. "Hey, you're supposed to be on my side."

The bartender threw the towel he had in his hand to wipe the bar down over his shoulder. "Hey, I'm neutral. I just listen to people remember." Then he walked away.

Getting back to their conversation, Marcus picked up his glass, took a swig of the bitter fluid, and then turned to Jim waiting for him to say something. Jim shifted in his seat not sure what to say. There was an eerie silence between the men as Cliff, Jim, and Marcus all sat listening to the music. They chatted a little and drank until closing time, and nothing more was said about Vanessa.

. . . .

Vanessa heard something in the far-off distance but couldn't quite make out the sound. Her eyes were heavy and she struggled to open them. A wave of nausea hit her as the bile made its way up her throat.

A chill came over her as a breeze ran over her body. She tried to move, and the restraints strained but didn't give. As the fog in her head began to disperse, her vision began to improve and she took another look around. There was nothing really in the room, but to her right Vanessa saw something with flashing lights. She strained her eyes further. It was some kind of machine. The sound she heard was coming from it. She recognized the sound now. It was a heart monitor. The rhythmic sound of the beep, beep, beep made Vanessa shiver. A frightening thought came to Vanessa's mind.

Oh god, I've been in an accident and I'm in the hospital. How stupid I am. I should never have left the university and driven in the dark. I should have gone back to my room and asked Marcus to meet me there.

Vanessa thought about that concept for a moment. If she had asked Marcus over she knew what would have happened. They would have ended up in bed together. That just wasn't an option.

Vanessa closed her eyes again. She heard a moan and the heart monitor paused. Vanessa shot her eyes open. Her vision was clearer now and she looked at the monitor realizing it wasn't hooked up to her. She breathed a sigh of relief. Then she saw who it was hooked up to. A knot of fear tangled its way through her like a vise grip. In front of her was a woman who, under different circumstances, would have been the epitome of beauty. She was attached to the wall by metal shackles that were used centuries ago in prisons. The electrodes stuck to her chest, and tubes came out of every opening in her body. Her chest heaved with every breath she took. Her naked, battered body was almost lifeless as it hung suspended like Jesus was to the cross, left to die. Vanessa watched fearfully at the scene that played out in front of her with wide eyes, a scream in her throat, and a sob in her heart.

Then suddenly she realized where she was. She was in the clutches of the mad man who had abducted and killed those women in the newspaper clipping, and the helpless woman in front of Vanessa was none other than Shyla Demone.

. . . .

Larry pulled the hatchet out of the sheath that was perfectly placed on his right hip. He slashed at any and all the branches that sat in his way. The moon shone down through the tree casting eerie shadows and playing tricks on their eyes. Randy stuck close to his nemesis, fearing the forest beyond more than the terror that Larry could bestow on him. The lights from the bonfire cut through the trees as sharp as Larry's hatchet. The drums reverberated off the forest and became louder with every step. Unconsciously Randy stepped in time to the beat, bobbing his head as he went. Getting himself into a methodical rhythm, the music became more hypnotic the closer they got. Suddenly Larry stopped and Randy walked right into him.

"For Christ's sake, Randy, what is wrong with you?" Randy looked sheepishly at him and shrugged his shoulders.

Larry pushed the bushes aside to get a better look at the scene unfolding around them. The bonfire rose to the heavens, licking at the sky with a fierceness Larry had never seen before. The natives danced around it bowing and swooping their arms as they went. They chanted words with conviction and pride, their wooden staffs raised to the night sky. Others grunted to the music, all becoming one entity as the energy swirled the far reaches of the rain forest. Larry and Randy looked at each other in amazement as some members took one man by the hand and led him to what seemed like a throne at one end of the camp. The man looked scared and on edge. He was dressed in full tribal gear that Larry recognized from some of the pictures he looked at in the board meeting.

"Hey, doesn't that look like the getup the medicine man was wearing?" Larry didn't take his eyes off the man.

Randy leaned forward and squinted. "Yeah, I think so. I read somewhere that only a child of the medicine man can take his place once he is dead. You don't think this is an initiation to bring in that guy's son, do you?"

Larry nodded. "It looks like it. Wow, that is great. We get to witness a real tribal ceremony. As far as I know no outside person is ever allowed to be a part of this stuff. It is punishable by death."

Randy slowly turned to look at Larry. "Are you fucking kidding me? We are sitting here incognito watching something we will burn in hell for!"

Larry chuckled. "No, but if we get caught we are done for."

As if on cue Larry felt something sharp at his back, and Randy shot to his feet and spun around. "We're dead!" Looking down at him was a mammoth of a man, his face intricately painted white and red. The other man was a little shorter but just as intimidating with his spear aimed at Larry's back. Larry slowly stood up and turned around, raising his hands in protest. The men grunted something and shoved them in the direction of the bonfire. Larry started walking, and Randy followed reluctantly but realized he didn't have a choice.

Randy's voice took on the fear he felt. "What do we do now, genius? We are about to be made into a midnight snack, and really I don't think there is enough of us to feed all these people."

Larry's usual confidence slipped away as they walked past the man they watched being brought to his throne and to the foot of what looked like an alter of some sort. Larry couldn't make out all the stuff that was on it, but it looked similar to an altar used in voodoo ceremonies. His stomach began to turn and his head buzzed with thoughts of how to get them out of this. The villagers began to gather around and talk amongst themselves. A man appeared behind that altar like a god, and all the villagers got to their knees and bowed. Randy looked around and wondered what that kind of power would feel like, having women from all walks of life bow at his feet.

Larry grabbed Randy's arm "We better get out of here before we get caught. These people deserve their privacy, they have been through enough already."

The two men crept back through the darkness undetected and made their way back to camp unaware of what was waiting for them.

Cooked spiders are a delicacy in some parts of the world. In the South Pacific they eat the same spider they use to weave fishing nets, and in Southeast Asia they fry them and sell them for a snack to passersby.

Chapter 11

The warmth of the sun on Larry's face brought a smile to his lips. He snuggled deeper in his sleeping bag, bringing the edges tight around him as visions of his dream were still fresh in his mind. He could feel the velvety softness of her skin under his fingertips. Larry opened his eyes to feast on the most beautiful sunrise. The various colors of orange, red, and fuchsia ran together like blocks of hot wax melting on a blue canvas. In the distance the cockatoos could be heard nattering to each other, and a parrot flew overhead. Suddenly Larry wished he could soar high above the treetops, in an endless flight, feeling the freedom of the wind under his wings. He thought of all the advantages. *Doing the fieldwork would be a whole lot easier. We could cover more ground.*

Larry unzipped his sleeping bag and stood up to stretch. Something pulled Larry's eyes to his left, and he turned to see what used to be their native guide. All that lay in front of him now was an intricately woven cocoon. Larry saw something move in the grass. He couldn't make out what it was, but it was moving rapidly away from them to seek the safety of the forest. Larry couldn't move, his voice failed him, and his legs were paralyzed with fear. He managed to get no more than a whisper past his lips.

"Randy ... Randy, wake up!" Larry shifted his eyes toward the sleeping bag that his fellow colleague occupied. It didn't move. Larry slowly shuffled his feet toward the bag. "Randy!" Larry lifted his foot and swung it, kicking at the sleeping bag. Randy stirred and awkwardly sat up rubbing his head.

"Do not tell me you just did that." Randy glared at Larry who was sheet white with eyes as big as saucers, still looking at the sight in front of him. Randy followed Larry's terrified gaze. Instant panic hit him as he jumped to his feet like a slingshot.

"Holy shit!" He stumbled back a couple feet. "What the hell is that?"

Larry could do nothing more than shrug his shoulders. The two men stood staring at the life-size cocoon, not sure what to do. Finally, Larry stepped toward it cautiously picking up a stick from the pile of starter wood they used for the campfire the night before. Holding it out in front of him, he walked closer.

"What the hell do you think you are doing?"

Larry jumped, startled by Randy's voice, and then whirled around to face him. "What does it look like I'm doing, asshole? We need to investigate. We need to know what it is and how it got here, don't we? We aren't going to find out anything if we stand here looking at it all day." He turned back again taking one more step.

"You can't just go poking at it! You don't know what could jump out of it at us." Larry stopped instantly, closing his eyes and gritting his teeth in annoyance, and turned once again with smoldering eyes. "So what do you suggest we do, dipshit?"

Randy stammered, shifting from one foot to the other. "I don't know, damn it! I just don't think it's a good idea to poke it. Where the hell did our guide go? Get him to do it. That's what we pay him for, isn't it?"

Larry rolled his eyes, turned back to the object, and pointed at it. "Moron, I think this *is* our guide." He walked around it slightly jabbing it with the stick, but nothing happened.

Randy went pale at the thought that it could have been him in that pod. "What could have done this?" He took a small step forward. Larry crouched down and lifted some of the substance with the stick. It wasn't a gummy, sticky substance that Larry thought it would have been. Instead, he found it to be like cotton. It was a webbing of some sort.

Larry looked up at Randy. "Well, what do you think?"

Randy was somewhat shocked that his colleague would ask his opinion, turned toward their gear, and flipped open one of the metal cases. He found what he was looking for and walked back to Larry. "First, we need to get some samples to take back to Cliff."

Larry smiled. "Finally, you're thinking on your own." Randy gave him a smug grin. The two men worked together for the next twenty minutes collecting various samples and labeling the vials. When they were finished, Larry reached into his knapsack and found his two-way radio.

"Larry to base, do you copy?" Larry waited for an answer but none was given. He repeated his words. "Larry to base, do you copy?" He let go of the button, the radio crackled to life, and a voice came over the radio waves.

"Base to Larry, I copy."

It was Cliff. Larry breathed a sigh of relief. "Hey, Cliff, you had me worried for a minute. Listen, we have a bit of a situation out here. Our vehicle broke down last night and we had to make camp." He paused.

Cliff's voice came to life. "Okay, I will send a replacement vehicle. What are your coordinates?" Larry read off the directions and then paused again. The radio crackled, "Copy that, Larry. I will have a team out to you by nightfall."

Larry pressed the button again. "Cliff, you might want to bring a second transport group. We have another situation that needs to be dealt with. You might want to tell Dunstan to send along some of his team too."

Larry heard Cliff clear his throat. "What kind of situation?"

Larry thought for a second about how to put it into words. "We have something Marcus and Vanessa are going to want to see. That's all I can tell you for now. You might want to get the team to hustle out here. I don't want this to decompose before we can get it to the university."

Cliff replied, "Copy that. I will get the team out right away. Maybe I should send a chopper as well."

Larry hesitated. "No, just a ground crew. A chopper will disrupt the area and we will lose the evidence."

"Copy that. We will see you when you get here." Then the radio went dead. Larry placed the radio in his bag and walked back to where Randy was packing up the samples.

"I saw something moving in the grass just before I woke you up. I don't know what it was, but judging by the way the grass was moving I would bet that it was a fair size."

Randy raised his eyebrow, and a shiver ran up his spine. "What? Thanks for telling me now, jackass." Randy nervously looked around. Larry looked around as well. "When the team gets here I think you and I should stay behind and gather clues as to what that could have been."

Randy shot up like a rocket. "Are you out of your bloody mind? I'm going back to the university where it's safe. I'm not sticking around to give this thing a second shot at me. You're the bug man. Why don't you go by yourself if you're so damn interested."

Larry glared at Randy. "You know we have to stick together as a team. We can't go out there alone."

Randy looked around nervously, not sure what he was looking for. "Well, maybe you should wait for Marcus. He should be here for this."

Larry showed no effort to hide the grin on his face. "You know, you could be right. At least it will get you out of my hair and I can get some work done."

Randy walked away and started to pack his things. "I think that is a splendid idea. Why don't you get Cliff on the radio and tell him there will be two passengers going back with them."

Larry was about to say something when he heard a rustling in the grass behind him. Turning slowly on his heels he scanned the area but saw nothing. "Randy, did you hear that?"

Randy was too busy rummaging in his bags. "I didn't hear anything but your fat mouth flapping in the wind." There was another rustling in the grass. This time Randy stood up and looked toward it. "Larry, over there."

Paralyzed, the two of them gazed on. Larry stood up slowly trying to get a better look. "Randy, come on, we have to go check it out."

Dumfounded, Randy retorted, "You're out of your damn tree. I'm not going anywhere near what's in that grass. You can see what it did to our guide. I'm not going to be the next one."

Larry glared at him. "But there is a chance that it will come and get you anyway."

Randy quickly thought about this concept. "You have a point there. I think we're better off together."

Larry rolled his eyes. "You're such a chicken shit."

The two men slowly advanced through the grass toward the unseen predator. The grass moved away from them at a quick pace.

Randy suddenly stopped. "Shit, wait a minute. We need something to catch it in." He turned and ran back, on wobbly legs, to the campsite.

Larry kept his eyes on the moving grass. Randy came back with a small cage, and they descended forward again. The predator stopped, and Larry gave Randy a signal to go around to the right, and he would go to the left and circle around. The predator sauntered forward as if unaware of the two men. Larry gave another signal to Randy, and Randy dove toward the creature and landed with a not-so-elegant thud with the cage still in his hands stretched out in front of him. Larry stared in total amazement and surprise as Randy gasped for breath and rolled onto his back. Larry carefully walked over to the imprisoned creature.

Randy gasped. "Did I get it?"

Larry let out a snort and then walked over to his winded colleague. With his hands on his knees he crouched down to gaze at a pathetic-looking Randy. Larry detained the gale of laughter inside him. "Are you okay?"

Randy, still gasping, grabbed Larry's arm in a desperate plea. "Did I get it, for Christ's sake?"

Larry looked over at the cage and snickered. "Yup, you did a fine job there."

Randy let go of Larry's arm and sighed. "Thank god!"

Larry offered Randy his hand and helped him onto his feet, and the two men walked to the cage. Larry slapped Randy on the back, and Randy winced. "Randy, my boy, if I ever need someone to catch me a good meal, I'll surely call on you."

A dumfounded Randy stared at the cage. Rage formed in his stomach as he took two steps backward and kicked at the ground.

"A rabbit! I caught a fucking rabbit!" He stormed around in circles cursing and venting his anger as Larry stood back and watched. The laughter he held could not be contained any longer.

Between gasps Larry tried to speak. " If you … could only see … how god damn funny you looked … flying through the air …" he panted. Trying to breathe, he flailed his arms around in the attempts to reenact Randy's procedure in the capture of his ferocious prey.

A not-so-impressed Randy watched as Larry went on. Seeing how ridiculous it all looked should normally have infuriated him more, but instead he laughed. He rubbed his chest as the two men shared the gale of laughter. Time seemed to stand still as Larry and Randy took part in a ritual that was thought to be impossible. It was a bond of sorts, which was only shared by friends. The two men sat on the ground across from each other with the cage in between them.

"Well, what should we do with it?" Larry asked as he reached into the cage and pulled out the miniature rabbit. He placed it on his lap and stroked the white fur and floppy ears.

Randy put the cage aside and gazed into its eyes. "You would make a good meal, but I think Larry would have a hard time eating you, so I think it is best if we let you go."

Struck by Randy's sudden act of kindness, Larry picked the rabbit up and looked at it face-to-face. "Man, you are the luckiest damn rabbit. He never shows his soft side. Hell, I didn't even know he had one. I think he hit his head so you better run while he still has a concussion." Larry gently put the rabbit on the ground and tapped its back end. The rabbit hopped away, stopping every once in a while to look back at the men. Randy sneered at Larry. "Ha ha, aren't you the comedian."

The men sat in silence for some time, enjoying their surroundings. The sun beat down on them, and the sounds of the jungle began to emerge. In the distance Lydia sat in a banana tree watching the two. An orange-breasted finch sat motionless on a branch below Lydia unaware of her presence. With elegance and an unhurried stride, she descended down the branch. Slowly she crept, one long cobalt blue leg after another, until she was no more than a foot from her prey. Gracefully she shot her intricate webbing toward the bird, capturing it in one fell swoop. The bird struggled with the webbing to no avail. Swiftly Lydia ran to the prey, sinking her horrendous fangs deep into the bird's fragile body and excreting the fatal venom that would result in death. The bird let out one last cry that cut through the forest like a bullet. Then ... silence.

Larry's and Randy's necks snapped toward the sound. A shiver shot up their spine, and fear escalated into terror as they remembered the predator was still very much alive.

Contrary to popular belief, spiders are not affected by pesticides. You have to close off all cracks in the house to keep them out. But since they like to eat termites, they might be a good species to keep around.

Chapter 12

$\mathcal{M}$arcus tossed and turned for most of the night and now lay staring at the ceiling with his hands tucked behind his head. His right cheek rested slightly on his perfectly shaped bicep. His fear gripping him, he racked his brain trying to figure out what could have happened to Vanessa the night before.

Cliff, Marcus, and Jim retraced the road that led to the university, making sure she hadn't run off the road or had car problems. Jim told Marcus that he hadn't seen any other cars on the road when he went to the bar. Marcus had a hard time believing him. There had to be someone going either way at some point. Marcus thought long and hard about the conversation they had that night. Jim was looking for someone when he came in and asked about Vanessa. Why? He looked almost panicked. Why? What did Vanessa have that she felt needed to be discussed last night? Why couldn't it wait till morning? Something just wasn't fitting, and Marcus knew Jim had something to do with it. He sat bolt upright and muttered under his breath.

"What if Jim had something to do with Vanessa not making it last night?" He jumped out of bed and began dressing. "If that bastard laid one finger on her head I'll—"

There was a knock on the door, and Marcus darted for the door, opening it so hard the wood cracked at the hinge. "Vanessa, where the—" His words fell off. Cliff stumbled back from the harshness of Marcus's reaction.

"Sorry, Cliff, I was just hoping—"

Cliff cleared his throat nervously. "Sorry to disappoint you, Marcus, but it's just me."

He smiled weakly. "You haven't heard anything either?"

Marcus looked down at the ground and moved aside so Cliff could enter. "No, and frankly I am getting worried. I've been up all night."

Cliff placed his hand on Marcus's shoulder. "I can tell. No offense but you look like shit." Marcus nodded in agreement as he caught a glimpse of himself in the mirror that was situated in the bathroom across from him. Cliff sat in the oversize chair in the corner of the room.

"I heard word from Larry about ten minutes ago. They need a team to go out there. I think they found something, but he wouldn't elaborate. He said it was, quote, 'a situation.'" Cliff raised his hands and made quotation signs in the air. "I'm not sure what that meant, but he sounded shaken. He wants Jim's team to go too, which I thought was weird, so I came right down to get you."

Marcus raised his eyebrow. "Huh, I wonder what that's about." Cliff shrugged his shoulders and Marcus continued. "It must be pretty significant if he wants a whole team there." He thought for a moment as he fought with the arms of his shirt as he tried to get his arms through. "God damn piece of shit." He threw the mangled shirt on the floor and walked to the closet for a fresh one.

Cliff looked on as Marcus struggled again with the hanger the shirt was on. Cliff stood up, giving his colleague a hand, reaching for the shirt, and helping Marcus get it on without tying himself in a knot.

"Relax, she'll surface. You know her. Maybe she met some cute guy and decided to get a piece of action." Realizing that might not have been the best thing to say, he stammered. "I mean … well … she … I"

Marcus glared at him. "Thanks for the pep talk, buddy, but you're not helping. Let's go." Marcus walked to the door, grabbing his briefcase on the way out.

· · · · · · · · · · · · ·

The team was busying themselves getting equipment into the large cargo van when Marcus and Cliff arrived on the scene. Jim Dunstan was checking off the articles on his list when he heard a voice behind him.

"What the hell is all this shit for?" Marcus wasn't impressed.

Jim turned to face Marcus. "Whatever do you mean?" The sarcasm in his voice was apparent.

Marcus shot a hostile look at Jim. "I am not in the mood to play games, Jim, and I don't see the point in taking all this stuff. It's just weighing us down and it's unnecessary. We don't even know what we are dealing with yet."

A student walked by pushing a large cart that carried spectrometers, retractors, scalpels, stereo microscopes, and various other instruments and headed for the ramp on the van. She smiled lovingly at Marcus, and Marcus cautiously smiled back turning his attention back to Jim. "Jim, we don't need all this."

"Excuse me? Of course we do. Like you said, we don't know what we are dealing with. We have to be prepared for anything."

Marcus groaned and thought to himself, *The only thing you have to be prepared for is keeping your sorry ass out of jail, dickhead.* He turned to Cliff, trying to do his best Shirley Temple imitation. "This is going to be so much fun." He put his middle finger on his cheek that was facing Jim. He knew it was immature, but he didn't care.

Marcus turned his attention to the team of students. "Let's hurry it up a little. I want to be out of here before next year, okay?" The students picked up their pace, and Cliff, Marcus, and Jim put their belongings in the Jeep that would be the lead vehicle. Marcus took one more look around with the optimism of possible seeing Vanessa come bouncing out of the university doors yelling at them for trying to leave her behind. She was nowhere to be found. Marcus turned to Cliff with no more than a whisper in his throat. "We are going to have to tell Randy and Larry that Vanessa's missing."

Cliff hopped from one foot to another nervously. "Do you really think she is missing?"

Marcus bit his lip. "I don't know what to think, Cliff, but I can tell you one thing. I really don't have a good feeling about it. If she isn't back by the time we are, I am going to call the police."

Jim couldn't help eavesdropping. He couldn't hear all of it, but he made out the words "Vanessa" and "police." That was all he needed to hear before he started to feel sick to his stomach. He could feel the blood drain from his face.

Marcus turned to see Jim's reaction. "What's the matter, Jim? Not feeling well?"

Jim turned to look at him. "Oh no, I'm fine. I sometimes get a little motion sick. I guess the anticipation of the trip is getting to me."

Marcus chuckled. "What, you? Well, you could always stay behind." There was a wicked grin on his face. Jim walked past him and brushed Marcus's shoulder. "Yeah right, in your dreams."

Cliff stifled a snicker at the boldness Jim showed. With tensions running high, the three men climbed into the Jeep and the team began their journey into the jungle beyond.

. . . .

Shyla opened her cumbersome eyes and tried to fight the nausea that threatened to overwhelm her. A scent filled her nostrils that she couldn't quite place. It smelled slightly of floral and musk, like cologne. She had smelled it before but she was not sure where. It was the first pleasant odor she had the pleasure of smelling since she began her torturous visit here. Straining to stay awake, she fought the effects of the drugs that invaded her body. She focused on the scent, fluttered her eyes, and then she heard a far-off voice. Not the voice she has gotten use to hearing, it was a gentle female's voice. Shyla's anger began to arise. *I must be hallucinating. Damn drugs. I wish he would just kill me and get it over with.* The nausea struck again. *What the hell did he give me? I hope the little shit comes over here so I can puke on him, and then sweet victory will be mine.* The voice began again. "Shyla … Shyla, can you hear me?" Shyla's heart began to race. *Oh god, she knows my name! Maybe I have been rescued. Oh, Jesus, please.* Shyla tried to move her lips and say something, but all that surfaced was an inaudible mumble.

Vanessa leaned as far as she could in her chair without falling over and tried to keep her voice at a whisper. "Shyla … Shyla, can you hear me?" She glanced at all the tubes and gadgets that were hooked up to Shyla and grimaced. *Shit! She must be in so much pain, but then again she is pretty drugged up. What the hell is Jim doing to her?* Vanessa looked around more to get some clues. Judging by some of the machines, Vanessa assumed he was just keeping her alive. What she couldn't figure out was why. All his other victims he raped and killed. She noticed Shyla was trying to open her eyes. Vanessa looked down the hall to make sure no one was coming and then turned her attention back to Shyla.

Shyla …Shyla, stay with me, honey. Come on, open you eyes. That's right. You're doing great."

Shyla fought to lift her head to no avail and then opened her mouth again, but this time her voice didn't fail her. "Where am I? How did you find me?" As she talked, saliva ran down her chin.

Vanessa felt a pain in her heart at the realization that Shyla thought she was here to rescue her. How could she tell this woman the truth? She let out a heavy sigh. Better to leave that part out. "Shyla, my name is Vanessa Thompson." She paused. "Can you see me?" Vanessa struggled with her restraints. Figuring it was no use, she began again. "Honey, keep fighting. Do you know what he gave you?"

Shyla shook her head. "No, the bastard was having too much fun keeping me guessing what his next move would be. Am I in a hospital? Where is my boyfriend?"

Vanessa didn't have the heart to keep the truth from her any longer. "No, I'm afraid. I wish I had better news for you, sweets. You are still …" The words caught in her throat and she paused. "I think I have been caught as his next victim, I'm afraid."

Shyla started coming around, and she opened her eyes again. Her vision was slightly blurred, but she could make out Vanessa's silhouette.

Painfully, Shyla lifted her head to rest it on the wall behind her. "Shit."

Vanessa snorted. "My sentiments exactly."

Shyla concentrated on Vanessa's facial features. The blur began to fade, and it came into focus. Vanessa's blonde hair was piled wildly on the top of her head and held with a clip that sported a beautiful golden phoenix. Her makeup was done to perfection, but her clothes showed signs of a struggle. Her dress was ripped up the front and partially hung like a rag. There were dirt smudges along her arms and legs. Small cuts trailed up her calves like she was dragged. Her shoes were gone, and her big toe on her left foot was smattered with dried blood. The rope around her ankles was attached to the legs of the chair that limited her mobility.

Vanessa followed Shyla's gaze. "I guess I'm not quite the welcoming committee you were hoping for." She looked down at her dress. "Damn, I just bought this dress too!"

Shyla, for the first time in days, chuckled. "Yeah, I don't think the asshole gave much thought to how much a woman's wardrobe means to her." Shyla looked down at her naked battered body. "At least you have clothes. I guess there's no sense in being modest."

Vanessa smiled weakly. "Do you have any idea what he's doing?" Vanessa pointed her chin toward the machines.

Shyla scanned the room. "Not really, he keeps me drugged most of the time. He doesn't tell me anything. You would think he would give me the courtesy of letting me know how he is killing me." She smiled. "I don't even know how long I have been here."

Vanessa sparked slightly at finally having an answer to something. "Well, I think I can help you with that one. It has been about a week, give or take a couple days. I saw a newspaper clipping about your disappearance."

Shyla nodded. "God, it feels like a month. How did Todd get you? Did he give you that 'Would you like to dance with me and make me the envy of the room' bullshit?"

Vanessa's confusion apparent on her face, she stammered, "I … I don't understand. You said his name was Todd."

Shyla nodded. "Yeah, Todd Davis. I met him in the bar in town. He was coming on to me, so I figured a dance couldn't hurt. Man, was I wrong. I should have stuck with my first instinct."

Vanessa started chewing on her lip. "Todd Davis? But that doesn't make sense." She looked up at Shyla. "What does he look like?"

Surprised by the question, Shyla answered, "You mean you haven't had the pleasure of seeing him yet? You must not have been here that long then. He is about five-eleven, football-type jock, brown hair, young kid, probably a college or university student. Why, do you know him?"

Vanessa thought hard. She remembered driving to the bar and getting out of her car and … nothing. She never made it to the door. Her head wasn't sore, so she couldn't have been hit. She was positive it had to be Jim who abducted her. He was the only one who had anything to gain from it. Just then she heard a scuffling of feet coming down the hall.

Shyla spat. "Speak of the devil himself."

Taylor turned the corner and walked over to the machines. "Oh good, you two have met." He turned and smiled at Vanessa. "I hate introductions."

Vanessa gasped. *"You!"*

Taylor turned, looked behind him, and then pointed to himself. "Who? Me? Oh yeah, surprise."

Vanessa snarled. "Taylor Lemay, if I recall."

Taylor let in a gasp of air. "Oh, how sweet, you remember me." He turned a couple dials on the machine closest to him.

Shyla shot a baffled look at Vanessa. "Taylor Lemay?" She looked at Taylor. "Of course, it is all making sense now. If you give me your real name I could escape and send you to prison, so you gave me an alias, Todd Davis."

Taylor laughed. "Sweetheart, you are in no shape to go anywhere, in case you haven't noticed."

Shyla started to remember something. "Hang on a minute … Taylor Lemay … that name sounds familiar … wait … it's coming." She reached far into her memory. "Yes, that's it! I remember you. You're that punk kid who got off on all those date-rape charges a while back. You have been the one who has been taking those university girls." She looked at Vanessa. "Yeah, that's it. This shit raped a few girls and got off on the charges and somehow managed to stay in school without getting killed. I bet you shut those girls up good. What did you do, threaten them?"

Taylor shrugged. "You have to do what you have to do to survive, darling." He began writing notes on his clipboard.

Vanessa frowned. "I'm still not sure if I understand this, and I'm not going to waste my time thinking about it. What exactly are you doing to Shyla?"

Taylor shifted his eyes to Vanessa. "Well, I wish I could tell you but—" He paused. "It's a secret but you'll have the pleasure of witnessing the whole thing. Aren't you so lucky? I mean I didn't plan it that way. I was going to bask in my brilliance myself but it seemed like too much fun taking you to pass it up." He winked at Vanessa, and her skin crawled.

"So are you going to do this to Vanessa too?" Shyla couldn't keep the anger in as she spoke.

"Oh no, not at all. This is all your glory and spotlight. The stage is all yours." Taylor bowed as if greeting the queen herself.

Shyla laughed. "What makes me so special?" Taylor didn't take any time answering her. "I have searched for some time to find you, my little butterfly." He ran his hand down her cheek. Shyla tried to turn away but there was nowhere to go. She snapped her head toward him attempting to bite his fingers.

Taylor jerked his hand away just in time. "Oh, baby, aren't you getting feisty." He growled excitedly. "Let's save that for later." He grabbed at his crotch to adjust himself. "Wow, you have me all aroused now. What am I going to do with this?" Taylor pulled his penis out of his pants and displayed it to both women.

Shyla spat at him. "Why don't you put it in my mouth so I can rip it off your pathetic body."

Vanessa got into the conversation. "Hey, that sounds good to me."

Taylor took a step toward Vanessa. "I bet you would love to have this in your mouth, wouldn't you? I bet it's been a while since you had a man." He began stroking himself. If it were any other time this might have turned Vanessa on but not at this moment.

Taylor looked down. "Well, I can't waste this, so should I flip a coin to see which one of you gets the honor of pleasing me?"

Vanessa snorted. "Like fucking you is a pleasure. I'm surprised that thing can even reach."

Shyla burst out laughing, and Taylor spun and raised his hand. The slap reverberated off the walls, and Shyla's head hit the wall behind her knocking her out. Vanessa winced and shied away.

"Oh shit, now look what you made me do, bitch." His eyes bore a hole in Vanessa's head. He walked up to her and crouched down, looking at her at eye level. He put his finger on her chin and turned her head toward him. Her eyes connected with his. He smiled wickedly and traced his finger down her neck. He jerked suddenly, and Vanessa's dress ripped in the middle, exposing her ample breasts. He ran his finger along her skin until it rested on the clasps of her bra. With one flick of his finger the clasp unfastened and Vanessa's breasts sprung free of their silky confines. At that moment she wished she hadn't worn that bra. It was easy access and wasn't meant for Taylor's hands.

He pushed the cloth away to get an unrestricted view. His index fingers traced the areolas of both breasts. A shudder ran through Vanessa, and she fought the urge to spit in his face.

"Very nice." He placed the nipples in between his fingers, and his penis jumped to life once more. An encouraged sigh escaped his pouting lips. "I have a gift for you, Vanessa. You'll love it." He reached into his pocket and pulled out a syringe. Vanessa gasped and fought against the restraints that held her to the chair. "No …please!"

Taylor took the cap off. "Don't worry, darling, this won't knock you out. It will just relax you a bit. I want you to be fully aware of what I am doing to you." He sunk the needle into her skin and she flinched. Within seconds she felt light-headed and out of control of her own body. Her limbs felt heavy and awkward, and her head lolled back and forth like an elastic band. She couldn't keep her head up, and her chin fell to her chest.

"There you go, that's better." He untied the restraints, and Vanessa collapsed in his arms. He picked her up and awkwardly tore off the dress and bra, leaving the black silk panties. Taylor roughly threw Vanessa over his shoulder and walked to the wall opposite Shyla. Standing Vanessa's wobbly body up, he placed the side of his body against hers to hold her in place and then raised her arm straight out along the wall.

"This is the tricky part." He grabbed the shackle and fumbled to lock it around Vanessa's wrist. He repeated the process until she was completely suspended on the wall. Her feet were flat on the ground, but her legs were slightly parted. She couldn't believe her eyes, and she blinked several times to try to bring some reality to what she was seeing.

Savagely Taylor took Vanessa's nipples into his mouth and suck feverishly.

His shaft rubbed on her stomach. His tongue ran a trail down the length of her abdomen to rest on the rim of her panties. He took the material between his teeth and pulled downward, revealing her open mound. His finger traced the outline of her neatly trimmed hairline. He shivered with anticipation; he couldn't control himself any longer.

Taylor stuck his tongue out and lightly ran it down until he found the one spot that women can't resist. Against Vanessa's wishes, he began to violate her the way no man should. She tried to resist but her body failed her plea.

His tongue lapped at the pink hot skin. Anger raged through her.

She felt the nausea flow through her with a vengeance. The unwanted heat soared through her veins, and her blood boiled with repulsion.

Taylor happily drank her juice as he stroked himself. Vanessa began to shake, and with a sudden burst she screamed with every emotion she could muster. "Stop! Get away from me!" Taylor jumped up and thrust his swollen member into her depths, feeling the blazing heat and tight walls. Vanessa squirmed and bucked, feeling the outer lips begin to tear.

Taylor jerked and manipulated his penis to its full extent. Vanessa felt the power behind his orgasm, and a pain shot into her. The pain was more than she could handle. She gasped for air, the room began to fade, and a blackened world of unconsciousness overwhelmed her.

Wolf spiders shed their skin many times as they grow to adulthood, and they live for many years. They will usually only bite if provoked.

Chapter 13

It was midday and the sun shone with intensity far brighter and hotter than Larry ever remembered getting in the city. The landscape was breathtaking, and Larry marveled at every small detail. There was a slight breeze that was welcomed by every inch of his sweat-laden body.

Randy was busily trying to build a makeshift tent to cover the cocoon out of long sticks and banana leaves. They both agreed the sun could speed up the decomposing process in the cocoon and should be covered until the team arrived.

Larry, other than taking in the scenery, was engaged in getting lunch ready. Both men worked quietly, not getting in each other's way. As every agonizing moment passed, Randy discovered new things he could do to pass the time quicker. Larry was content just writing his notes and looking over his paperwork.

By four o'clock, Randy started pacing around the site. "What the hell is taking them so long? It didn't take us this long to get out here."

Larry looked up from his work. "How would you know? You slept most of the way."

Randy glanced at the cocoon. "It might be the only sleep I get for a while." He shivered despite the hot sun. He pointed to what used to be their guide. "Have you thought about what Shmingy went through in all that?"

Larry sputtered a laugh. "Shmingy? What the hell is a Shmingy?"

Randy looked at Larry with indifference. "I don't know. I just made it up. I can't pronounce his real name so I gave him a nickname."

"Huh, interesting. No, I haven't thought about it. I don't care to think about it. The thought is not my first priority." Larry turned back to his notes.

Randy started pacing again. "Man, I wonder if it was painful. I mean shit, who knows what did this to him. I'm just surprised we didn't hear it and wake up." Randy crouched down to get a better look. "He didn't even scream or yelp or anything. Maybe he didn't see it coming, you know?"

Larry was barely listening to Randy as he rambled on and on. Randy glared at Larry. "Hey!"

Larry looked up with a start. "What!" he said annoyed.

Randy stood up. "Did you hear anything I said?"

"No, not really." Larry smiled.

"Well, piss on you then!" Randy sat down with a thud, misjudging the distance between his butt and the ground and falling a little harder than he intended.

Larry sighed loudly. "Look, Randy, all I can tell you is it appears that it was some sort of spider obviously. What kind, I haven't got a clue, but it was big so it had to be in the tarantula family. I have been looking over some notes about the species around here, but it could be any of them. What I don't get is how fast it worked to get this meticulously weaved over night. Especially of this size." He thought for a moment. "Plus, why didn't it do anything to us?"

Randy shivered again. "Hey, better him than me. Maybe it doesn't like my blood type." He laughed nervously, half joking.

Larry said in a belittling voice, "No creature in its right mind would suck your blood." He smiled.

"Hah, that's very funny, porky. They would love you. They could feast for months." Randy pointed to Larry's protruding stomach.

Larry was about to retaliate when a sound caught his ear. Trucks were rounding the bend in the distance. Randy shot up and brushed the dirt off his jeans. Larry put his books down and stood up as well.

. . . .

Cliff pointed out the window. "There they are."

Marcus turned the wheel and headed toward the pair standing

and waving their arms frantically in the air. "I'm surprised they're still together. I figured one of them would have killed the other by now." They pulled up next to Larry and Randy.

Cliff saw the mound on the other side of the camp. "Well, I wouldn't count your chickens yet, Marcus." Cliff pointed to his findings.

Jim's eyes bulged. "What the hell is that?"

Marcus turned off the engine and opened his door. "Let's go find out." He walked over to Larry. "Glad to see you two are in one piece."

Larry put his hand on Marcus's shoulder and shone a toothy smile. "I have to tell you it has been trying at times." He turned to Jim and shook his hand. "Hi there, Jim. We have quite the job for you here." They walked over to the cocoon.

Jim gave a low whistle and circled around it a few time before settling in a crouched position. He waved for his team to move in and get set up. Instinctually, Jim put his hand out to touch the webbing.

Randy spoke up. "Ah, are you sure you don't want to put some gloves on or something?"

Jim didn't even look at him. He was too enthralled in the site before him. "The webbing itself wont hurt you. It's just a casing for the victim inside. It is nothing more than a protective coat so that other animals can't get at it before she gets back." Jim was mesmerized.

Marcus rose an eyebrow. "She?"

Jim didn't notice the question posed to him. "The web keeps predators away so she can come back to feast later." He took a sample in the glass tube that a student handed him. Jim handed it back to him, and he placed it gently into the rack of test tubes that sat beside him.

Larry crouched beside Jim. "It's from the tarantula family, isn't it?"

Jim looked at Larry with pride. "Yes, it is." He smiled happily. Marcus's eyes narrowed. "Ah, excuse me. You said 'she.' How do you know that? We haven't even done any tests yet."

Jim slowly gazed up at Marcus and cautiously spoke. "Yes, *she* is a cobalt blue tarantula, and she is hungry. She probably hasn't eaten in days."

Marcus, Larry, and Randy looked at each other in disbelief. Randy finally spoke. "You mean to tell us you know about this?"

Jim stood up and sighed deeply. "Yes, I do. I haven't been completely honest with you."

Marcus's heart started to beat faster and his face turn bright red. "You son of a bitch! I knew we couldn't trust you! You better start talking before I decide to not give you a chance." He took a step toward Jim, and Randy grabbed his arm. Marcus glared at Randy and backed down.

Larry stood up now. "Marcus, beating him to a pulp isn't going to help us right now. Wait until we get this all sorted out and then you can do as you will. I might just help you." He looked back at Jim and waited for him to speak.

"You have to admit, it is fabulous workmanship she has created here." He beamed as he stared at the cocoon.

Randy's anger built. "Who the hell is *she* you keep referring to?"

Jim sat down on the grass and offered a seat to the three men. They apprehensively sat down to face Jim Dunstan. He nervously started telling them the story. "Her name is Lydia, and I created her." Marcus was about to say something, but Jim put his hand up to silence him and continued.

"I have been working with DNA samples for a couple years now, and I wanted to see if human DNA could cohabit in a tarantula. I chose the cobalt blue tarantula because of its strong demeanor. They are an aggressive species ... a beautiful species. They are a dying breed and are sought out to be bred by people from all over the world because of their spectacular color. The cobalt blue is an aggressive but delicate spider, and if it is not meticulously taken care of, it dies. If this happens the species will become extinct in a couple of years. I mixed the DNA of a female cobalt and a female Goliath tarantula along with human DNA." He took a profound breath and looked at the men in front of him.

Larry was nodding his head in total agreement, but Marcus leaned forward and rested his elbows on his knees, glaring viciously. "And?"

Jim continued. "I started a case study. I used the cloning process and took the human DNA and the spider DNA, joined them, and came up with a super species."

"Brilliant! Absolutely brilliant!" Larry slapped his knee and beamed at the rest of the team, who unfortunately didn't feel the same. He suddenly felt uneasy. "Well, I can't lose sight of the fact that tampering with nature is a precarious decision on his part but, damn it, as a biologist I have to appreciate it for what it is, and that is absolute brilliance."

Marcus rolled his eyes and turned back to Jim. "So what happened to your invention? She just got up and walked out on you, or what?"

Jim looked down at the ground pondering what to say. "As a matter of fact … yes."

Randy convulsed. "What! What! You mean she is out here somewhere? Holy fuck, man! It was her that did this?" He pointed with a shaky hand toward the cocoon. "Oh shit. There is some mutant fucking spider within a half-mile of us, and you decided to tell us now! You knew about this before we left the university and never said a damn word!" He turned to Marcus. "If you don't kill him I sure as hell will!"

Marcus could empathize with Randy's anger because he felt it too, but the rational side of him knew there was nothing that could be done about it now. He started putting the pieces together. "So you couldn't find her yourself and lied to the dean and everyone else, making it sound like it was some epidemic, and had them fly us out to clean up your mess. Am I getting close, Dr. Dunstan?" Everyone heard the malice in his voice.

Jim looked up at him. "Something like that."

Marcus smiled despite himself and snickered. "You're a real piece of work, aren't you?" Jim cleared his throat uncomfortably. Marcus kept going. "So while you are into a hiding secrets kind of mood, why don't you tell me where Vanessa is too?"

Larry snapped his eyes to Marcus. "Vanessa? What are you talking about? What's wrong with Vanessa?" Randy too looked at Marcus with questioning eyes. Marcus's gaze never left Jim. "Why don't you ask him?"

The two men turned to Jim Dunstan, who suddenly felt like he was part of a deadly inquisition. "What … what do you mean?"

Marcus snarled. "Don't give me that shit. You damn well know what I am talking about, asshole. I think it is interesting how Vanessa called me up last night and told me that she had something important to tell me and to meet her at the club and she didn't make it. But low and behold you show up looking a bit ashen and nervous. Sounds to me like you have something to do with her disappearance."

Shocked at the allegations, Jim pointed to himself. "Who, me? Are you crazy? Why the hell would I have anything to do with Vanessa last night? I told you I came there to unwind. I even recall asking you about her."

Marcus stood up and walked to the Jeep to grab his briefcase and then walked back. He opened it and pulled out Jim Dunstan's file, throwing it in his direction. It landed at his side, and Jim picked it up and looked at Marcus confused. "What's this?"

Marcus motioned for him to open it. "Please, be my guest."

Larry looked at Cliff and then Marcus in a daze at the news that Vanessa was missing. "Marcus, what is going on?"

Marcus turned to his team. "It seems that we have a felon in our midst. Jimmy boy is a convicted rapist! The mayor also happens to be Jim's father. It also seems that Dean Hursh owed the mayor a favor, and that favor was to give his beloved son here a job in the university. A convicted felon, especially a murderer, I would imagine would have a real hard time getting a job." He turned to Jim and forged a smile. "Don't you think?"

Jim's face was ashen, and his hands began to tremble. No more than a whisper touched his lips. "Where did you get this?"

Marcus smiled at Jim's panic-stricken expression. "That doesn't matter. What does matter is that I have a team member missing, and you seem to be a prime suspect."

Jim's students continued with the gathering and storing of the cocoon, oblivious to the tête-à-tête going on behind them. They all went about their business, all accept one who couldn't help but overhear. Joyce McGaver was standing by the Jeep performing a test on the samples they gathered, half listening to the men talking. Her heart began to pound in her ears and her breath came in short gasps. She couldn't have heard that right. Dr. Dunstan was a rapist? She dropped the vile that was in her hand, and it landed on the hard terrain, breaking into pieces and launching the fluid inside all over her lab coat and tan jeans. The men turned with a start and gazed upon her ghostly white skin.

Jim jumped to his feet and ran to her side. "Miss McGaver, are you all right?" He grabbed her arms and looked at her, concerned. Larry began delicately picking up the glass off the ground.

Joyce instinctively jerked her arms away from him and stammered. "Ah … yes … yes, of course. I just … I … well I … got the mixture wrong on this test and I ... I panicked. I'm so sorry, Dr. Dunstan, I didn't mean to ..." Her words faded off as she looked down at the ground. Suddenly she crouched to help Larry.

Jim gently took her hand and stood her up, taking the glass shards from her. "It's okay. Why don't you go clean yourself up. We can handle this."

Joyce couldn't look him in the eyes. She promptly spun on her heels and headed for the cargo van.

Jim whirled around to face Marcus, fighting to keep his voice subdued. "I don't know who the hell you think you are bringing this up here. I have worked very hard to right the wrongs of my life, and I don't appreciate you digging up my past in front of my students. I don't know what happened to your friend, and I will not stand here and let you blindly accuse me of being involved with whatever has taken place! I admitted to a hell of a lot today, but I will not be blamed for something you have fabricated in your jealous egocentric head. Furthermore, my past and present standing at the university are frankly none of your business. You are here to do a job, not snoop into my history!" He took a step closer to Marcus and glowered furiously into his eyes. "You are treading on thin ice, Dr. Tolson, and I would advise you to back the fuck off!" Abruptly Jim stormed off to the cargo van.

All Marcus could do was smile.

Most spiders live for one year, but some can live for three or four years. Certain tarantulas are known to live for twenty-five years.

Chapter 14

Vanessa awoke to sore, stiff muscles and a horrific headache. She was cold, disoriented, and her hunger pains were prominent. She felt the bile eating at her stomach lining. Opening her eyes, she looked toward Shyla. Shyla was looking at her with tired eyes. *How long has she been unconscious?* As if reading Vanessa's mind, Shyla answered, "Hey, sleepyhead, how do you feel?"

Vanessa tried to move, but her restraints held. "Like a Mack truck hit me. How about you? He hit you pretty hard." Vanessa winced as she attempted to stretch her cramped muscles.

"I'm getting used to it. What happened after I got knocked out? Wait ... maybe I don't want to know." Shyla quickly scanned the area.

Vanessa shook her head. "I wish I could remember. The last thing I do remember is—" She looked down to see her naked body. "Christ!"

Shyla attempted a weak smile. "Don't worry about it, honey. We're all women here."

Vanessa's foggy memory started to come in flashes and bits of scenes. She saw Taylor holding a needle. She remembered feeling pleasure, but how? How could she feel pleasure toward a cretin like Taylor Lemay? The thought sickened her, and she fought the bile that threatened to overwhelm her once again.

Shyla's concern showed on her face as she spoke. "Honey, are you okay?"

Vanessa was suddenly brought back to reality by her words and looked up at her detained companion. "I don't remember a whole lot, but what I do remember I wish I didn't." There was a distasteful twist of her mouth.

Shyla smiled halfheartedly. "I know how that goes but—" Her words caught in her throat. She began involuntarily gasping for air. Her eyes bulged from the pain she unexpectedly felt in her chest and stomach.

Vanessa squirmed in an endeavor to free herself. "Shyla, talk to me! What's wrong?" Vanessa stopped struggling, aware that the attempt was futile. Absolute fear seeped its tendrils deep into Vanessa's body as she watched the horror unfold. Shyla's stomach began to pulsate and stretch outward slightly, and then an agonizing scream escaped her lips. Vanessa screamed as well. Then, before her voice could betray her, she called out to the only person that could help Shyla. "Taylor! Taylor, you motherfucker, get in here! Something's wrong with Shyla!" She paused for only a second. "Taylor! I know you can hear me, asshole!"

Shyla's thunderous moan deposited shear panic into Vanessa. "Taylor Lemay, you scum-sucking pig! Where are you?"

What seemed like an eternity passed before Vanessa heard footsteps running down some stairs to her left.

"I'm coming. I'm coming." Taylor flew around the corner so fast he lost his footing. Slipping on a piece of plastic that was loosely hanging from the wall in the hallway, he slammed hard into the door.

"Shit!" He regained his composure and fiercely looked at Vanessa. "Jesus Christ, woman! What the hell is wrong with you? What is so damn important?" He rubbed his shoulder.

Under other circumstances Taylor's little misfortune with the door would have pleased Vanessa immensely, but she realized she would have to gloat later. "You idiot, it's not me. It's Shyla!"

Taylor suddenly looked panicked himself. He shot a glance toward Shyla and then at the machines beside her. Disbelief hit Vanessa like a shot to the head as she saw a smile come across Taylor's lips. A dangerous anger rose from the depth of her soul. Her voice took on a malicious tone.

Her words were slow and controlled. "What … the hell … are you … smiling at? Aren't you going to help her, you sick fuck?"

Taylor didn't bother to look at Vanessa but instead gazed lovingly at Shyla. He walked over to her side and brushed a strand of hair away from her painfully exhausted face. "Have patience, my love. I know this isn't easy on you. It will all be over soon and then—" He smiled and walked toward Vanessa. "And how are you feeling, my pet?"

Vanessa wanted to spit in his face, but her mouth was so dry she couldn't garner enough saliva to do so. "What do you care, pig? What are you doing to her?" Vanessa swung her chin to point at Shyla.

Taylor ran his finger along the underside of Vanessa's arm, and she instinctively shivered. "Well, it is a complex process that I am sure you would understand, seeing that you are in the field, but I really don't have time to sit and explain it to you. Sorry, dear." He turned, pushed a few more buttons, and then turned to the machine that controlled Shyla's intravenous.

"There, sweetheart, I set the machine to give you some Demerol every five hours. Do you want a little something to help the nausea?" He put his finger on the button, waiting.

Shyla nodded despite herself. "Please."

"I want this to be as comfortable as I can make it for you." He smiled.

Shyla stuck her middle finger up at him using all the energy she could muster. "Why don't you at least let me have some idea of what you are doing so I can be a good patient for you, pissant."

Taylor smiled at her lack of humor. Thinking for a moment, he placed his hands on his hips. "Well, what I can tell you is." He paused. "You are going to make me a very happy man." Then he walked down the hall.

Vanessa looked at Shyla, who looked exhausted and vanquished. She glanced down at Shyla's now-protruding belly. Then she started putting some pieces together to make sense of what has transpired. *He raped her and got her pregnant. That has to be it. But it takes nine months to give birth, and Shyla is transforming too quickly. Your stomach doesn't just grow like that all of a sudden. What the hell is he doing? Come on, Vanessa, think, think, think.* Her thoughts came in flashes. She started remembering old biology lessons and dismal speeches that she sat in on. One in particular that she actually enjoyed was the cloning process. The words of her professor played in her mind:

"Cloning is the process of creating identical offspring using a single cell or tissue. Cloning doesn't give exact copies, but the ordinary person would never know the difference. To give you the long and the short of it all, they started testing cloning on frogs and then mice. The unfertilized cell was melded together with a uterine cell of the frog or mouse, therefore producing an embryo that is inserted into an adult surrogate mother."

Vanessa watch as Shyla's abdomen moved slightly.

"Some argue the pros and cons of the cloning process, but I believe cloning could revolutionize science, as we know it today. Just imagine, if you will, all the proud parents of the world never having to worry about defects to the unborn child. They could eliminate the possibility of passing on a genetic disease, such as dementia or diabetes, to the child. Although at this point in the game it is debatable. There are also arguments about the making of a perfect human down the road."

Vanessa looked at Shyla. "I think I know what he is doing to you."

Shyla fought to lift her head and apprehensively look at Vanessa. "How could you possibly know what he is doing?"

"Because I am a biologist, and Taylor Lemay is a student at the University of Peru."

Shyla, stunned by Vanessa's words, tried to make some sense of it all. "How do you know him?"

"I was brought to Peru with my team to figure out why some of the tribesmen in the jungle have been dying recently. I was investigating one of the professors at the university when I found some files, but that's another story. I think Taylor has impregnated you with his child and sped up the incubation process. Why, I'm not sure yet. Unless he is trying to get a jump on the human cloning process." She thought for a second and then continued. "You see, scientists are trying to get the cloning process down to an art before they start cloning humans. People think the process is too inhumane to be tested on people yet. There is way too much controversy for the government to fund such a thing. I think Taylor is trying to bridge the gap. I mean, what better way to do the testing without being funded or getting caught?"

Shyla shook her head. "You mean to tell me I am a human test tube?" She began to feel movement in her stomach. "Oh god, I feel the baby inside of me." She started to cry. "I never thought I would be a mother this way." Fear gripped her. "What if it comes out deformed or something? What will he do to it when it is born? That fucker better not use it as a lab rat!" The movements felt gloriously strange. She began to relax and enjoy the euphoria of a first-time mother even if it wasn't the way she planned it. She smiled. *My baby will be beautiful,* she thought. The painkillers kicked in as she drifted off to sleep.

. . . .

The Peruvian police were already at the university when the team arrived that night. The lab that they had been working in was being picked apart down to the last piece of paper by a squad of about five men in blue coverall-type uniforms with matching berets. Marcus looked around at the crew in astonishment and noticed the dean talking to a man who Marcus figured had to be the leading detective. He walked over to the men and cleared his throat to get their attention.

The dean turned. "Oh, Marcus, I'm glad you're here. This is Detective Pablo Triscot." The dean made a gesture toward the detective, and Marcus offered his hand to greet him.

Marcus turned back to Dean Hursh with a frown and a facetious tone to his voice. "Can I ask what's happening here, or is it classified information?"

Neither the dean nor the detective gave in to the joke. Instead, the detective straightened his back and, with a sturdy look, cut to the chase. "I got an anonymous phone call to my office today from the university. She said something about a lady by the name of Vanessa Thompson going missing last night. We are here to look into the accusations, Mr. Tolson." The detective motioned to the dean. "Mr. Hursh has told me that she is on your staff. Is that correct?"

Marcus was too stunned for any sentence beyond a quiet "yes." His thoughts came in flashes. *How did anyone know about this? I'm not even sure if she is really missing.*

The dean put his hand on Marcus's shoulder. "Marcus, I'm so sorry to have to break it to you this way. I thought she went with you and the team this morning." He sighed. "I have no clue who phoned the police, but I am looking into it. I'm getting Gertrude to call the phone company to get records of any call that went out and came in yesterday and today. Hopefully that will help."

The team now stood beside Marcus. Cliff's white skin gave away what he was feeling, and Larry's shaky hands fell on Cliff's arm. "Let's not get ahead of ourselves here. Just because someone makes a call and claims to know Vanessa is gone doesn't mean it's really hard evidence.

It could be some woman that is playing a practical joke, for all we know." Larry didn't believe it as he said it either, but it sounded better than the alternative.

The detective glanced at Larry with suspicion. "Are you telling me that she isn't missing, Mr. …?

Larry held out his hand. "Dr. Larry Schultz."

The detective took Larry's hand. "If she wasn't missing, why wasn't she with your team this morning? Don't you all travel together?" He looked at Marcus.

Marcus frowned. "No, not always. Two of our team went out on field duty two days ago, and the rest of us stayed here. I don't really think I need to explain protocol with you, do I?" He looked at the dean. "Do I?"

The dean looked embarrassed. "Of course not, Marcus, but we need to find out what is going on. It's probably nothing, like Larry said, but we can't take any chances, can we? Can you tell us what you know?"

Marcus looked around at the disaster the police were making in disgust. "Well, unless you are going to charge one on my team with kidnapping, I suggest that you call off your hounds here. They're going to destroy any chance of finishing our project. Did you bring a warrant to pick apart our stuff?"

The detectives' narrow eyes told Marcus not to push the issue. After all, they weren't in New York, and he didn't want to land his ass in jail in a foreign country. "Are you objecting to my team helping your friend? Do you have something to hide, Dr. Tolson?"

Marcus didn't like his tone and was losing his patience. "Oh, for Christ's sake! No, I don't have anything to hide! But you're tampering with my work here, and I really don't want to have to start over again if one of your inept squad fucks something up!"

The dean cleared his throat and turned to Marcus. "Please, Marcus, they are only trying to do their job. They will be done as soon as possible, and then you can get on with your work. I'm sure Vanessa is just sightseeing and lost track of time. Maybe she stayed in town for the night and forgot to call you."

Marcus swung around to glare at the detective. "If you want to point fingers at someone, why don't you start with Jim Dunstan? I'm sure he has plenty to say!" Then he stormed out of the room.

Lydia

The dean shook his head with disappointment, and the team stood with dumbfounded looks on their faces. In the far corner behind a mobile blackboard hidden from view stood an ashen Jim Dunstan.

. . . .

Marcus walked to the truck that carried the equipment and explained to the students how vital it was for them to store the equipment and the cocoon in a separate lab so the police didn't tamper with it. He then helped them with the unloading. Joyce McGaver slowly walked over to Marcus and placed her hand on his arm. "Excuse me, Dr. Tolson, may I have a word with you?" Her eyes carried a solemn stare as she looked into Marcus's eyes, and Marcus shivered despite the hot sun. Her fair skin looked even paler than normal, and she had tears in her vibrant green eyes. Her hands were cold, clammy, and shaking. Marcus took her by the shoulders to hold on to her just in case she fell to the ground.

"My god, Joyce, are you okay? You look like you're going to pass out. Do you want me to call Dr. Styne to take a look at you?" Marcus led her to the grass beside the parking lot, sat her down on the curb, and then made himself comfortable beside her.

Joyce released her grip on him and sank to the ground with ease. Her stomach, once queasy, now relaxed, and Joyce melted as Marcus put a caring arm around her to hold her steady. In a normal circumstance this would have sent her to the moon. She had many fantasies about the icon, Marcus Tolson, whom she knew so much about. She made a point of learning all she could about him and followed in his footsteps, taking the same course load he had taken when he was attending the university. She almost couldn't contain herself when she found out Marcus was coming back to Peru and that she was going to be working with him and his team. Her best friend Angie listened endlessly to Joyce's ramblings about how she wanted to be as successful as he had been, and one day she would meet him and possibly join his team. She never dreamed it would really happen, and now he was here touching her. She gazed into his eyes and fantasized for just a fraction of a moment what it would be like if he leaned in to kiss her.

"Joyce, are you okay? The color is coming back in your face so you must be feeling a little better." Marcus released her and she came back to reality like a bullet.

"Okay … Yeah, I'm fine. I need to talk to you about something very important though." She looked around to see if anyone was listening and then whispered, "In private." She looked down and started wringing her hand nervously. "It's about your friend Vanessa Thompson."

The Australian crab spider sacrifices its body
as a food source for its offspring.

Chapter 15

Vanessa fell in and out of sleep restlessly, listening for any sign that Shyla might be conscious. Shyla, from what Vanessa could tell, had been out for a couple hours. Judging by the temperature change, Vanessa figured it had to be sometime in the evening.

She drifted to a time when she saw Marcus at the university in New York where he was giving a lecture on the life cycle of the praying mantis.

She hadn't seen him in years, since they studied at the University of Peru together.

The lecture hall was packed and she was lucky enough to have left early to get a seat in the second row. The stage was set up with cages and props and a table full of pamphlets, brochures, and pins.

She remembered Marcus coming out onto the platform to start his speech, wearing a praying mantis hat as well as sporting a set of large wings attached to his back. Eyes bulged on both sides of his head, and the wings bounced joyously as he walked across the stage.

The roar of laughter was deafening as the students and professors lapped up Marcus's enthusiasm for his lecture. Marcus gazed out at the crowd and stepped up to the microphone.

"Oh, you think this is funny, do you? Well, I have a little something in store for you too, my pets." With a wave of his hands the back doors opened up and a team of people came marching out down the aisles with their arms full of hats for the crowd.

The hats contained the heads of caterpillars, flies, crickets, aphids, butterflies, moths, and more. Marcus beamed as he heard the gasps, awes, and gales of uncontrollable giggling.

Two blonde cheerleader-type girls were trying to grab them to get at the butterfly hat that was in Vanessa's hand, so Vanessa decided to keep that one for herself and passed on the fly, aphid, and moth hat to the two horrified-looking teens.

Vanessa smiled smugly and stuck out her tongue in a not-so-mature fashion as she plopped the hat on her head and then gazed down at Marcus.

"I'm glad to see that you all approve and are willing to participate without too much grumbling. You all get to keep the hats as a constant reminder that—" He pushed a button and the overhead projector came to life. The words came into view larger than life in bold red letters that said: you are my prey!

The laughter slowly died away, and the control was back in Marcus's hands.

"The praying mantis feeds on insects like you to survive. As for all you men out there, just when you thought you had women all figured out and think that you had control, guess what?" He walked over to the middle of the stage with the microphone in his hand. "Just like the mantis, they mate with you." His voice took on a deep, low, malicious tone. "Then they eat you!"

The crowd went wild. Women stood up clapping and screeching, and the men, taking it out of context and making it very sexual, stood up hooting and hollering with suggestive undertones. The guy who sat in front of Vanessa stood up, turned around to push his pelvis toward her face, and said, "Yeah, baby, come eat this! That's right, you know it!"

Vanessa raised her eyebrow. "Baby, you couldn't handle it!" Marcus cleared his throat and tried to get the crowd to calm down.

"Okay, okay, let's get down to business." He began the two-hour speech, and after it was all finished he had teenage girls pushing and pulling to get to the stage to get his autograph. They asked him to help place the praying mantis pins on their shirts, and he was more than happy to oblige. Vanessa watched the scene in front of her and had to laugh under her breath. When the students filed out of the hall and no one else was there, Vanessa finally stood up and walked to the stage. Marcus was taking off his wings and hat and packing the paperwork into his briefcase. Vanessa stood behind him unknowingly to Marcus.

He stood up very slowly, almost cautiously, and cocked his head to one side. "I do believe I have an unseen predator at my back. What could it be?" He turned to gaze on the most beautiful woman he had ever seen.

Her hair was a mass of long blonde waves that flowed freely over her golden tanned shoulders. Her blue eyes shone with the brilliance of the soft satin, her lips parted slightly to pearly white teeth.

Marcus steadied himself against the urge to reach out to her.

"Hello, Marcus, remember me? I thought your lecture was fascinating and humorous." She took the hat off her head. "And I love the hat. Thank you." Marcus's smile lit up the room, and Vanessa knew she was going to fall in love with this man all over again.

A sudden buzzing filled Vanessa's ears, and she shot back to the present. The intravenous machine's alarm was going off to tell them that the bag needed to be changed.

Shyla groggily began to move, her stomach now protruding—by normal standards it would be approximately eight months along. Vanessa was glad that Taylor was at least companionate enough to keep her sedated so the pain didn't bother her too much.

Taylor came around the corner, turned off the machine, and then changed the bag of fluid that hung on a hook on the wall beside Shyla. He placed his hand on Shyla's belly and rubbed gently, smiling to himself, and then turned to leave.

Vanessa coughed. "Taylor, could I please have some water?" She long ago learned that she would get better results if she was civil to him. Taylor stopped and turned to face her. "Yes, of course, precious. I'll be right back."

Vanessa's mouth was so dry and her body was so battered that she didn't have the energy to fight him. Taylor had inserted an intravenous in her arm when she was drugged up, but it didn't seem to be enough. She felt like she had eaten half the dessert.

Taylor came back with a glass of water with a straw in it. "Here you go, this should help." He placed the straw in her mouth, and she drank feverishly, not sure if she would get anything more for some time. When she was finished she nodded to Taylor and took a breath.

"Thank you." She wasn't sure how to ask her next question but decided to take a chance. "Taylor, how much longer until Shyla gives birth?"

Taylor was astounded by the inquiry. "Well, it won't be much longer. A few days at most." He turned to Vanessa. "So you have figured out what I am doing?"

Vanessa nodded slowly. "I think so, but what do I have to do with all this? Why am I here?"

Taylor smiled. "Like I said, Vanessa, you were a bonus. I don't have any plans for you. I got caught up in the moment and wanted to watch Marcus Tolson sweat a little trying to find you. It's great. I have classes in the morning and get to watch what is going on, and then I come here in the afternoon to take care of you two. That way I get to keep an eye on everyone. So far no one knows you're missing—well, sort of. I can sense Dr. Tolson is wondering why you didn't make it to the bar. The plan couldn't work any better really." He smiled. "If all works out the way I am hoping it will, your lover will take care of Jim Dunstan for me. Once he is out of my way, I am home free to reap the rewards."

Vanessa frowned. "You men are all alike. You use women to get what you want." She looked over at Shyla. "So once you have what you want, what are you going to do with her and me, kill us?"

Taylor's grin broadened. "Oh, that is already planned out. Don't you worry." Then he turned and walked away.

Vanessa's heart sank at the thought of never walking out of this building again. She had so much she wanted to do yet.

Telling Marcus how she really felt about him was at the top of the list. A shiver caught her off guard. That feeling of being watched filled her fears once again, as it did in the boardroom that day.

Her eyes scanned the room to see if Taylor was there. She saw nothing but felt the presence lurking. In the corner of her eyes she saw a movement, maybe a mouse or rat. Vanessa squinted to get a better look. Nothing. She took a breath. Whatever it was disappeared. She closed here eyes again and tried to relax. Suddenly she heard something to the right side of her head about a meter off. Panic struck her and fear gripped her chest. She couldn't open her eyes; instead she squeezed them tighter as the sound of it came closer. Vanessa couldn't stand it any longer, and she opened her eyes wide. In her peripheral vision the movement was closer than she thought.

By pure instinct her head swung toward the movement. There in its enormity sat the biggest tarantula Vanessa had ever seen. The body alone was at least two inches in width and the legs were approximately four inches in length. Its hair shone the brightest blue, and the underbelly was the deepest black.

Lydia sat staring at the woman, her body motionless but tense with fear. Lydia lifted her leg and slowly placed it on Vanessa's hand. She could feel the woman's pulse quicken as the blood pumped faster through her veins.

Vanessa felt a scream come from the depths of her, but it wouldn't come out. As Lydia looked into her eyes, Vanessa had a sudden feeling wash over her as though she could trust the tarantula that sat beside her even though her fear ran wild through every inch of her body.

Something told her that this creature was not going to hurt her. When the spider placed its massive blue and black hairy leg on her hand, Vanessa felt a calm wash over her. She couldn't explain it nor would she try for fear that she had finally lost her mind.

"I guess you wouldn't happen to have a hairpin on you? I would sure like to get out of these shackles." Vanessa smiled. "I guess not."

Lydia removed her leg and then backed up slowly. With one more glance she turned and scurried away.

. . . .

Marcus agreed to meet Joyce at a local coffee shop that night so they could talk privately. He had no idea what she wanted to talk about, especially since it pertained to Vanessa. As Marcus drove to the coffee shop, his mind began to wander. *Was she the one who called the police? No, that can't be because she was with the team at the site. What does she know?* Marcus pulled into the parking lot and parked the Jeep. He saw Joyce waving frantically at him through the window. He walked to the table and sat down. "Hi."

Joyce beamed. "Hi." She couldn't believe he was sitting here with *her.* "I'm glad you made it."

Marcus ordered a nonfat cappuccino with a splash of mint and cinnamon sprinkled on top. He always thought it was a girly drink until Vanessa got him hooked on it in New York. The waitress left, and Marcus turned his attention back to Joyce. "Okay, so what is this all about? What do you know about Vanessa?"

Joyce took a deep breath and scanned the room nervously. "I overheard you talking to Dr. Dustan at the site today. You were blaming him for your friend's disappearance. You said that he was a rapist in the past and all that." She took a sip of her coffee.

Marcus was taken aback. "You heard all that?" Marcus suddenly remembered Joyce dropping the test vile. "Is that why you dropped the vile?"

Joyce blushed. "Yes, I couldn't believe what I was hearing. Dr. Dunstan has been my professor for three years. I haven't known him to hurt anyone. He barely even raises his voice in class." She nodded. "It was a bit of a shock."

The waitress came back with Marcus's coffee, and Joyce waited for her to leave to continue. "Dr. Tolson, I don't believe Jim Dunstan has anything to do with Vanessa Thompson's disappearance."

Marcus took a sip of his cappuccino and looked at her with concern. "You can't know that, Joyce. You don't know his past. I do. So what do you think happened then?"

Looking uncomfortable, Joyce began playing with the stem of her cup. "You're right, I don't know his past, but I do know something about the rapes around the campus, Dr. Tolson, and that is why I asked you here. I called a friend of mine on my cell phone when we were at the site. I told her what I overheard, and she called the police to make an anonymous call to tell them about Vanessa's disappearance. I had assumed you hadn't called them yet, and I didn't want to take the chance that you would wait for her to just suddenly show up."

Marcus's head was swimming. "What are you talking about? No, I hadn't made a decision yet, but if she hadn't shown up when we got back I was going to call them. I don't really think it was any of your concern to get yourself involved in this."

Joyce looked at him with pleading eyes. "Dr. Tolson, it is my concern. It is every girl's concern on this campus. There have been quite a few date rapes going on in the last few months, and the asshole is getting away with it. It's time it stopped."

"What do date rapes have to do with, Vanessa?" His eyes narrowed and his eyebrow rose as he leaned into the table toward Joyce.

"Dr. Tolson, none of the girls were willing to come forward to bust this guy because he would threaten them. Now that your friend has gone missing, it has the whole campus scared."

"Word really travels fast, doesn't it? So you girls think that this guy has taken Vanessa? But you don't think it's Jim Dunstan. Am I getting this right?" Marcus took another sip of his coffee.

Joyce fidgeted with her ring. "That's right. My friend was one of his victims, and she is terrified that if she comes forward he will kill her. But I talked to her and she is willing to talk to you to tell you her side of the story."

Marcus now was the one fidgeting. "Well, okay, then tell her to come with you to my room and we can talk there."

Joyce looked at him horrified. "Are you nuts! She will be caught for sure. Dr. Tolson, I hope you don't mind, but I took the liberty of setting this meeting up so you could talk to her now."

Marcus suddenly felt as though he was caught in a trap. "Now?"

Joyce smiled. "Do you want to find your friend, or what?" She turned to look toward a table in the corner where a single girl sat. Joyce nodded at the girl and she rose up and walked apprehensively to their table and sat beside Joyce.

"Dr. Tolson, I would like you to meet my best friend Angie Styne." The girl held her hand out to Marcus, and he took it. Angie was an average-looking girl with auburn hair and dark blue eyes. The circles under them told Marcus that it had been a long time since she'd slept. She was shaken and nervous and jumped at any sound around her.

"Styne? As in Dr. John Styne?" The girl in front of him nodded sorrowfully. Marcus sat back, not sure what to say. "Now I understand why you didn't want to come forward. Does your father know, Angie?"

Angie took a shallow breath. The words came out in a whisper. "No, sir. Joyce is the only one who knows, and now you do too. Joyce says I can trust you, so that is the only reason I agreed to meet you. I'm sorry about your friend." She looked down at her lap, and Joyce reached over and held her hand.

"Dr. Tolson, Angie is willing to help you find your friend, but you have to agree that she will not be exposed."

Marcus let out a low whistle. "Angie, I'll do what I can, but you really should tell your parents. Your dad can get you the help you need to get past this and get on with your life." His concern deepened.

Angie shook her head and then looked into his eyes, which was something she hadn't been able to do since the rape. "I can't tell him.

It's better this way. Joyce is my strength. She is all I need." Joyce smiled at her friend.

"Do you want to know who did this?"

Marcus held his breath and nodded. For the next hour he listened to the story and watched as both the girls blotted the tears that streamed down their faces. Angie told him about the fateful night that she was grabbed on her way back to the campus from a frat party and brutally raped, beaten, and left in a gutter on the side of the road, the disbelief in finding out she was pregnant, the traumatizing ordeal of having to leave the country to have an abortion, and then the healing process after the doctor butchered her womb so bad that she would never conceive again.

When they were finished, they stood up and Angie spoke one last time. "Dr. Tolson, I want you to catch that bastard and make him pay for everything he has done to all the girls on campus. I want Taylor Lemay put in jail for a long time." Then they were gone.

Marcus was left feeling numb from the shock and visual horror of Angie's story. He was sickened and mortified that anyone could ever do that to a woman. Remorse overwhelmed him as a tear ran down his face. He suddenly felt ashamed to be a man. He watched the girls walk to Joyce's car and drive away.

Neither one of the girls noticed the dark blue Jeep that followed them out of the parking lot.

Joyce turned the corner and took a deep breath. "Well, how do you feel about the conversation and Dr. Tolson?"

Angie fidgeted with the zipper on her jacket and contemplated her answer carefully. "I think he is really nice, and he seemed to really be listening to what I had to say. I feel for him though. You can totally see the pain in his eyes and his heart about Vanessa's disappearance. He must care about her a lot."

Joyce felt a pang of jealousy find its way into her soul. "Yeah, I suppose so. Wow, that car behind us is wavering all over the road. He must be drunk or something."

Angie turned in her seat and looked out the back window, squinting to see it in the dark. The headlights shone brightly in her eyes and then veered to the oncoming traffic. As the car pulled up to the side of Joyce's little Honda Civic, the Jeep seemed monstrous in comparison.

"I guess he is going to pass us. What an asshole. He's going to kill someone if he keeps …" Joyce's words stopped as the Jeep came closer to her car, forcing her to swerve toward the ditch. "Holy shit!"

Angie screamed as her body slammed against her door and her head hit the window. Joyce quickly corrected and brought the car back to the pavement. The Jeep sped off up the road and disappeared. Joyce's hands were shaking so badly she could hardly steer. "What the fuck was that!"

Angie rubbed the lump on the side of her head. "I don't like this, Joyce. Something doesn't feel right."

Joyce tried to calm her nerves by taking deep cleansing breaths. "Don't worry about it, Angie. It was just an idiot that was in a hurry and felt like being a dick. Man, it takes all kinds. Angie just couldn't seem to shake the feeling that this was intentional. Her fear suddenly took hold and she realized talking to Dr. Tolson was a big mistake.

The weight of insects that spiders have eaten every year is greater than the total weight of the human population.

Chapter 16

Jim sat in his office wondering how he had gotten into the mess that was unfolding in front of him. How did Vanessa slip past him? He was right behind her until … he wasn't sure when he lost sight of her. He turned into the pub just as she did. He found a parking spot, got out of his car, and she was gone.

How could she just disappear without a trace? He wasn't going to hurt her; he just wanted to know why she broke into his office. She had photocopied something from his filing cabinet, made a call, and took off to the bar. The call was obviously to Marcus, and Marcus hid it quite well. Now he was getting blamed for her disappearance. Why? He hadn't done anything wrong since …

He couldn't think about that now. He had to help the team find Vanessa and then concentrate on getting Lydia back. He also had to get himself back to some normality.

There was a knock on the door, and Jim jumped. "Come in."

Marcus opened the door and poked his head in. "Hi. Are you busy?"

"No, not at all, unless of course you came here to pick a fight." Jim tensed slightly.

Marcus chuckled and walked in, closing the door behind him. "No, I'm not here to pick a fight. I need to talk to you."

Jim sat up straight and relaxed but still kept his guard up. "Not a problem. Sit down. Do you want some coffee? I just made it. It's a lot better than what the dean's secretary makes." A wide grin swept across his face.

Marcus laughed out loud. "I should hope so." Despite himself, he shivered. "Sure, I'll have a cup."

Jim got up and walked over to the table that served as a makeshift kitchen, poured them both a coffee, and then brought it over to Marcus. "So what shit am I in now?" He sat down and looked at Marcus.

"Actually, you're not in any … yet. I have to be honest and tell you I messed up and pointed the finger toward you when I was talking to the cops last night. I was pretty angry and I needed to vent, and unfortunately I came flying at you. I'm sorry."

Jim's eyes narrowed, and his hands began to sweat. It wasn't in Marcus's nature to say he was sorry for anything, and Jim knew it. "Why the sudden change of heart?" He felt like a scorpion was at his back ready to strike.

Marcus could sense Jim's apprehension and concern. "It's okay, Jim. You can relax. I know you didn't have anything to do with Vanessa. Furthermore, you're right. I had no business digging up your past. But I would like to hear your side to that if you are willing to talk about it to clear the air. It will stay between us, I can promise you that."

Jim took a deep breath and let it out slowly, almost painfully. "I really don't know what to tell you, and to tell you the truth I don't know what you are asking for." Jim sat back sipping his coffee and waiting for an answer.

Marcus thought for a moment. "I had a serious talk with someone last night, and I guess I want to know what was going through your mind when you raped that woman. You violated her in a way that only a monster could, Jim. I need to understand this because Vanessa is out there somewhere, and I don't know what is happening to her. I got a lead on who might have taken her, and I need your help. You were once in this guy's shoes, and I was hoping to get in your head so I could figure out what to do next to find her." Marcus tried to keep his emotions in check.

Jim looked down at his cup and studied the black fluid, a million thoughts coming into his head all at once. He suddenly didn't know what to say, and everything he wanted to say seemed so cold and callous. He glanced up at Marcus and saw the pain in his eyes.

"You must love her a lot to want to dance with the devil to find her." He bit his bottom lip.

Marcus raised his cup to his lips and then stopped. "Are you saying you are the devil?"

"All I am saying is that you are asking me to delve into a part of me that I have long forgotten. But I understand that desperate times need desperate measures. I'm just not sure how getting into my head is going to help you."

Marcus thought carefully about his words. How could he explain what he had heard last night from the girls? He had to try. "Well, I had a chat with one of your students last night, Jim. Actually, she came to me. She told me about all the girls on campus who have been date-raped and that none of them would come forward to convict the guy who did it."

Jim started to tense. "You better not be telling me you think I'm the one who did it."

Marcus raised a consoling hand. "No, Jim, you're not the one. I know that. What I am about to tell you has to stay between us, okay?"

Jim nodded and then relaxed once more. "Joyce McGaver overheard our conversation at the site yesterday and heard me accuse you of taking Vanessa. Joyce came to me and set me straight about that. She is a great kid who respects you and put herself in the line of fire to protect you. She said that one of her friends was willing to come forward and help convict the guy and help us find Vanessa, but she has to stay anonymous. I'm not sure how we can do that, but we will have to talk to the detective for that, and I figured since your father is the mayor, maybe he could pull a few strings for us."

Jim took a drink of his lukewarm coffee and then asked the question that was nagging at him. "Who is this guy?"

Marcus put his cup down on the desk. "If I remember correctly, he also is a student of yours. His name is Taylor Lemay. Vanessa bumped into him the day we arrived. He seemed to have quite an interest in her."

Jim dropped his coffee but managed to salvage the cup. The warm fluid poured all down the front of his pants. "Son of a bitch!" He stood up, walked to the coffeemaker, and grabbed a cloth to wipe his pants. "Are you out of your fuckin' mind, Tolson! Taylor is one of my best students. What proof do you have? What, just a couple of girls who have it in for Taylor? They're probably pissed off that he didn't ask them out on a date, for Christ's sake. He has a great career ahead of him, and you are about to take him down. He could end up being better than you and me put together, Marcus."

Marcus watched as Jim tried his best to clean his now-stained pants. "Jim, the girl who came forward was one of his victims …" He paused and then continued. "She is also Dr. Styne's daughter."

Jim stopped what he was doing to look at Marcus in shock. "What? Are you sure?"

Marcus nodded but said nothing else. Jim walked over to his desk and sat down dumbfounded, forgetting to wipe the seat that was also full of coffee. He cursed again and then abruptly felt the wind being knocked out of him. Confusion set in like a mass fog invading his mind. Marcus finished his coffee, put his cup down, and then looked at Jim. "Styne doesn't know about it, Jim, and it has to stay that way or she won't help us. There's a lot more to this story. That's why she wants to stay unseen, but that is between her and her soul. It's not for us to try to fix."

Jim sat quietly and listened to Marcus. His head was swimming and his stomach was turning. "I've known Styne for years. I watched Angie grow up." He ran his hand through his hair. "My god, how could this have happened? Why didn't she come to someone?" He was talking to himself more than to Marcus.

Marcus leaned forward. "The same way that you attacked your victim, Jim."

Jim snapped out of his sudden hell and glared at Marcus. His voice was low and threatening. "What happened with me wasn't premeditated; it was …"

Marcus raised his eyebrow. "Go on." He looked at Jim with a challenge in his eyes.

Jim sighed. "When I was in my early twenties I was dating a woman who turned out to be from a rich family and had the upbringing of the higher-class citizens. We fell in love and wanted to marry, but her family didn't think too highly of me. I came from a middle-class family and her father wanted her to marry in her own class. On the advice of her father she started acting holier than thou and telling me that I wasn't good enough for her and that my performance in the bedroom was less than adequate."

Jim blushed slightly. "We did nothing but fight after that. One night she came over to my place telling me she loved me and she just said all those things because of her father. Of course I figured that one out already. She said she wanted me to make love to her that night and prove how much I loved her. She said she wanted to run away with me. So I did as she asked. I ran her a bubble bath and made love to her all night."

Jim smiled. "She loved me. I could see it in her eyes … so I thought. That night I asked her to marry me, and the next thing I knew shit hit the fan. She started yelling at me and hitting me in the face, saying that I could never be good enough for her, that I was a second-class fool and why would she want to marry someone like that." He looked down at his hand that now started to shake.

"I raged. I pinned her down on the bed and held her arms down to get her to stop hitting me, and then she stopped struggling. She started telling me she was sorry and that I was the only love she knew and that she was scared. My head was swimming. I didn't know if I was coming or going. She said she wanted me to show her how bad I wanted her. She lifted her legs and wrapped them around my waist and told me to make love to her again. I was so mad I thought that was it, that I was going to show her how a real man does it. It got a little rough, but she seemed to like it. The next thing I knew I had the cops on my doorstep arresting me for rape." He stopped and looked at Marcus with a tear in his eyes.

"I didn't rape her. It was a ploy to get me out of the picture. Her father was a very powerful man. One word from him and I was put away for five years."

Marcus felt a pang of guilt for judging Jim before he knew the whole picture. "Jesus, Jim, I'm sorry. I had no idea."

Jim nodded. "Yeah, well when you have that kind of label on your head, that is all people see. So on a different note, tell me more about Angie Styne and let's see if we can get to the bottom of this." The men sat for the next couple hours making a game plan that hopefully would catch Taylor and save Vanessa.

. . . .

131

Detective Triscot sat at his little desk trying to make sense of the papers in front of him. He needed more coffee to get his brain to work because he had been up most of the night looking at the Vanessa Thompson case. There wasn't one lead that he could go on, not even a hair sample. It was like she vanished in thin air. Her car couldn't be found, and there wasn't a single piece of evidence to say there was a struggle in the bar parking lot, not even a witnesses. One thing was for certain, though, and that was that Vanessa Thompson must have known her abductor. He stood up and walked to the coffeemaker in the main area that held the police force together. It was like the heart of the force: filing cabinets, computers, and the best damn coffee in all Peru.

Lieutenant Rivera hollered from the front desk. "Triscot, there are a couple guys here that want to talk to you. They say it's about the Thompson case."

The detective nodded. "Send them in." He took his mug back to his cramped office and cleared the two chairs in front of his desk for his visitors.

Marcus Tolson and Jim Dustan walked in led by the lieutenant who was at the front desk.

"Well, gentlemen, what can I do for you today?" Triscot got up and closed the door behind them.

Jim looked at Marcus, and then Marcus cleared his throat. "We have a lead on the case about Vanessa that we thought you might want to hear."

Triscot smiled with an edge of annoyance. "The last time I checked this was my investigation, and if I do remember correctly, Mr. Tolson, you were accusing Mr. Dunstan of being the perpetrator. Now you are both in my office telling me he isn't. Interesting."

Jim's smile matched Triscot's. "With all due respect, Detective, I was never a suspect, just a man caught in the middle. We have reason to believe that one of the students at the university is the one who took Vanessa Thompson. We have a woman who is willing to come forward to testify as long as she is kept anonymous."

Triscot chuckled. "Is that so? And what gives you the idea that she is telling the truth? Does she have proof?"

Marcus leaned forward. "As a matter of fact, she was one of his victims, and so were a few other girls on the campus. So far she is the only one who is willing to come forward."

Triscot thought for a moment. "Okay, tell me what you know. Then I will do some digging of my own and see what I can come up with. For now all you two can do is sit back and not make any waves. If what you say is true, we don't want to spook the guy and make him run. We need to find out where he goes and see who he talks to. I'll let you know when I find out more."

Marcus nodded. "Thank you. I appreciate this." Marcus told Triscot what he could about the conversation he had with Angie. When he was finished, Jim and Marcus stood up, said their good-byes, and walked out of the room. When they were out of the building, Marcus turned to Jim. "What do you think? Do we just sit and wait or do some digging ourselves?"

Jim smiled with a maliciousness that Marcus couldn't ignore. "Well then, I guess that settles it. Let's go find Taylor Lemay, shall we?"

The two men walked back to the car and headed for the university.

. . . .

Taylor walked down the hall toward his next class, smiling to himself at the thought that Shyla was close to giving birth. His head swelled with anticipation, for the last couple years he had worked toward this moment. The whole morning he couldn't keep his mind on his studies, and his best friend was wondering where he had been. Taylor was to meet up with Bobby Roe in the courtyard and walk to class together.

"Hey, man, how's it hanging? I've been looking for you all over campus, dude. Tom thinks you're, like, hanging with a new crowd or something." Bobby bounced over to Taylor like a dog would to his master. "So what gives?"

Taylor gazed at his pathetic friend and tried to think of something to say that wouldn't fry Bobby's brain into overload. "I'm working on a home project for lab class."

Bobby cocked his head to one side. "Like, what kind of project? Hey, do you want some help? I could bring over a couple six-packs and some joints, and we can get ripped. That'll get your creative juices going."

Taylor shook his head and put his hand on Bobby's shoulder. "Dude, I would really like that but I need my brain cells for this one, and I need to do it alone. It shouldn't take more than a couple more days. Then I can spend some time with you and the guys, okay?"

Bobby looked hurt, but then he smiled. "Okay. Hey, maybe we could round up some chicks and have a party and get a piece of ass." He laughed and snorted loudly.

Taylor looked around embarrassed. "Okay, we'll do that. Hey, I have to get to class. I'll talk to you later."

"Okay. Hey, Taylor, did you see all the cops around here last night? Something about that hot babe you were talking to the other day went missing."

Taylor pretended to look indifferent. "What babe?"

Bobby smiled. He knew that Taylor was a major chick magnet and talked to tons of girls and couldn't possibly keep track of any one of them.

"You know, that professor babe that flew in from New York with Dr. Tolson."

Taylor smirked at his friend. "Oh yeah, right, the one with the tight little body that can catch a football."

Bobby chuckled. "Yeah, that one. The word around campus is that she disappeared the other night and that Dr. Dunstan is a suspect. Go figure. You just never know who is teaching at this school, eh?"

Taylor grinned again. "Yeah, I guess so. I gotta go. See you later."

Bobby waved frantically as Taylor jogged away.

A spider doesn't stick to its own web because of the oils in its body, and a moth doesn't stick because of scales on its body.

Chapter 17

The lab was pretty quiet. No one on the team really wanted to talk much. Randy, Cliff, and Larry were busy tending to the tests on the cocoon when Marcus and Jim walked in. Marcus smiled at the gloomy faces that were staring back at him. "Hey, cheer up. We are going to find her, Jim, and I have a lead."

The men stared blankly back at Marcus, and then Randy spoke. "I thought you two hated each other, and Jim was the guy who took Vanessa in the first place."

Marcus's embarrassed gaze took on a crimson glow. "Yeah, well, don't believe everything you hear. I can make mistakes too, can't I? Look, it was all a misunderstanding and it's been rectified. There is a student in this school that apparently is the real suspect. I want you guys to go on about our business like nothing happened, okay? Jim and I are going to see what we can find out, and if anyone asks you anything—"

The guys said in unison, "We know nothing."

Marcus smiled. "We'll be back later."

Jim and Marcus left the room, and the team went back to their work with a little more hope than a few minutes before. The two men walked through the courtyard toward the cafeteria, stopping along the way to say hello to some of the other professors who were talking amongst themselves.

A short, gangly-looking man greeted Jim and held out his hand. His hair was thin and fluffy, like a cotton ball blowing in the wind, and his hands were very skeletal showing his age. "Well hello, Dr. Dunstan, how are you on this fine day?"

Jim took his hand and shook it firmly. "Hello, Dr. Watkins, I am doing just fine, and how are you? I hear you have some fine students graduating this year that will make us all look good."

Dr. Watkins laughed heartily, beaming all the while. "Yes, yes, I have to say I have a good crop this year. I just wish we could have students like this every year. Although I think I am getting too old to keep up to them, some of them really give me a run for their parents' money. I think I'm learning more from them." He turned to Marcus. "Well, isn't this a pleasant surprise, young Marcus Tolson. I hear you have grown to be quite the biologist in the big city."

Marcus shook the man's hand. "I can't complain, Dr. Watkins. It's been a long time since I saw you last."

Dr. Watkins nodded in agreement. "Yes, it has, dear boy. I remember you sitting in the back of my class with all your arrogance, not paying any attention to me, and putting all your attention on one Miss Vanessa Thompson." He looked over his spectacles, showing Marcus that his body might be failing him but his mind was very much functional. "I also heard about her recent disappearance." His face took on a sorrowful tone. "I'm so sorry, dear boy. I'm sure she will show up "no worse for wear"

Marcus nodded. "I'm sure she will, Professor."

The elderly man patted his shoulder and then turned back to Jim. "Well, I must be off. My class is about to start. Have a good day. Oh, and try not to fight about any woman. God, you two fought something fierce about that Thompson girl." As he walked away, he muttered to himself, and neither Marcus nor Jim could hear what he was saying, but what they did hear stunned them both.

"What the hell was he talking about?"

Marcus, with eyebrows in a frown, looked at Jim, who smiled. "You really don't remember do you?"

Completely dumbfounded, Marcus blankly gazed back at Jim, shrugged his shoulders, and tapped his temple with his finger. "Nope, nothing in my noggin."

Jim wasn't sure if Marcus was kidding or not but preceded anyway. "I can't believe that. You do remember that we went to this school together, right?"

Marcus started to walk, and Jim followed. "I actually don't, but the dean said something about it. Why? What do you remember?"

Jim shoved his hands deep in his pants pockets. "Well, I remember a frat party, and I sure remember Vanessa being there, and then I remember something about a jealous, drunk-as-a-skunk Marcus Tolson punching me in the jaw for talking to her."

Marcus stopped in his tracks and stared wide-eyed at Jim. "What! Yeah right."

Jim chuckled. "You broke my damn jaw, asshole. You had your overgrown hoodlum friends drag me out of the frat house bleeding and broken."

Marcus laughed out loud. "Holy shit, are you serious? I honestly don't remember, but then again I don't remember a lot of those years. When I wasn't studying I was drinking. Man, I'm sorry. I guess I was a little overprotective about her."

Jim laughed too. "I don't blame you. She was … I mean she is a pretty amazing woman. Don't worry, Marcus, we will find her." For the first time Marcus looked at Jim in a different light, almost the way a friend would look at another friend. "I'm praying, and I'm not a religious man."

The men walked the rest of the way in silence.

. . . .

Angie Styne lay quietly on her bed in her dorm room with her books spread out in front of her, like a fan, consisting of charts and scribbled notes. A bowl of popcorn sat at her side and a soda within her reach. Her temples throbbed as the words in front of her began to blur and her concentration began to fade. She closed her eyes for a moment, stretched like a cat, and then sat up to reach for the popcorn when there was a knock on the door. She picked up the soda, taking a sip as she walked to the door and turned the knob. The soda fell from her hand and a gasp escaped her lips as she came face-to-face with Taylor Lemay. She stumbled back as he pushed his way through the door before she had a chance to realize what was happening and closed it gently behind him.

"Hello, precious." He smiled maliciously. "I thought we might have a little chat."

Angie's breath caught in her throat as she tried to speak.

Taylor put his finger to her lips. "Shhh, I will do the talking, if you don't mind. I saw your little nosy friend talking to Dr. Tolson yesterday, and I wanted to remind you about my promise to you if she or you say anything about our secret. You do remember the promise, right? Or do I have to remind you?"

Angie's body shook as Taylor drew her close to him and glared into her eyes. She shook her head violently, and he let go of her.

"Good, because I really hate repeating myself." He walked over to her bed, flipped the pages in her book, and then picked up the report that she had been working on for the last two weeks, ripping it to shreds. "Oops, looks like you're going to have to start all over. What a shame. Well, I must be off." He got up and started for the door. Angie watched him with tears in her eyes, not turning her back on him.

"Next time it will be your throat I rip apart." He opened the door and walked out.

Angie ran and locked the door and then crumpled on the floor in a devastated, terrified mass, pulling her knees up to her chest in a fetal position and crying uncontrollably. After thirty minutes she slowly picked herself up off the floor and went to the phone. "Joyce, I can't do this. He is going to kill me." She dropped the receiver back in the cradle and lay on her bed sobbing for the rest of the day.

. . . .

Larry gazed through the microscope lens and turned the dials but didn't really have his mind on the specimen he was looking at. He couldn't concentrate on anything other than Vanessa's disappearance. His stomach ached and his anxiety rose as the minutes passed by. The door behind him swung open and smashed against the wall, making the team jump. Joyce McGaver burst through the door panting to catch her breath.

"Where is Dr. Tolson? I need to see him right away!" She steadied herself against the door.

Larry went to her side. "He went out with Jim Dunstan. They didn't say where they were going. What's wrong?"

"I need to see him *now*! It's a matter of life and death!"

Larry looked at Cliff and Randy and then back at Joyce. "I'll see if he has his cell phone on." He walked quickly to the phone in the corner of the room and dialed the number. Cliff took Joyce by the hand and sat her down on a stool. "Can I get you some water or something?"

Joyce shook her head. "No, thank you. I just need to catch my breath. Then I'll be fine."

Larry put down the receiver and walked over to the girl again. "You're in luck, he did have it on. He and Jim are on their way. They shouldn't be long. They're in the courtyard."

Joyce's breathing came back to normal. "Good."

Randy, now standing with the group, looked at Joyce scowling. "What the hell is so damn important that made you almost take the door off?"

Joyce scowled back, "You'll have to take it up with Dr. Tolson. I don't have time or the energy to tell you the story."

Randy raised his eyebrow. "Well, aren't you a testy little one." He was about to say something else when the door flew open again and Marcus walked in with Jim right behind him.

"Joyce, what happened?"

Joyce looked at him with tears in her eyes. "Taylor threatened Angie again. He went right in her room and threatened her life and said that if she or I talk to you he will kill her. He saw me with you yesterday afternoon. We have to do something. She won't even answer the phone. She didn't go to any of her classes today and hasn't left her room."

Jim looked at Marcus. "We better call the detective."

"Okay, you call him. I'm going to go with Joyce and see if I can't get Angie to open the door." Marcus took Joyce by the arm and walked out of the room while Jim went to the phone.

Larry turned to Jim. "Will somebody tell us what the hell is going on?"

Jim turned to face the team. "We know who has Vanessa. It's one of the students in my biology class. His name is Taylor Lemay, and we are working with the police to track him down and find Vanessa before it's too late."

Cliff muttered under his breath, "If it isn't already."

Larry shook his head in distaste. "I knew that kid was trouble."

Jim dialed the number of the precinct and waited for someone to answer. He tapped his foot impatiently. "Hello, yes, I am looking for Detective Triscot. Well, interrupt him, damn it, this is urgent. Yes, I'll hold." Jim tapped his fingers on the table and then lifted his head and gazed out the window. Suddenly, he spotted Taylor Lemay walking to the parking lot toward his car. "Shit!"

He handed the receiver to Larry. "Tell him what you know, and tell him to call Marcus for further information."

Larry took the phone nervously and yelled back to Jim, "Where are you going?"

"I have to follow Taylor before he gets away!" Then he was gone.

Jim ran across the driveway to the parking lot and found his car. As he fumbled with his keys he watched Taylor pulled out and drive off the university grounds. Jim unlocked his door, jumped in the car, and then pulled out of the lot himself. He made sure there was enough room between him and Taylor and then picked up his phone to call Marcus. "It's Jim. I'm following Taylor. It looks like he is going out of town. I'm about a mile out. I got Larry to call the detective. I'll call you back when I know where he is going." Jim hung up and concentrated on the road. "We've got you now, asshole."

Taylor turned left down a dirt road and slowed down, unaware of the car behind him.

A well-known myth about the Daddy Long Legs (harvestmen) is that it is the most poisonous spider in the world, but it can't kill anyone because its jaw is too small to bite anyone. This is completely false. It is not poisonous at all, and there is no evidence to suggest that its bite is harmful to humans.

Chapter 18

Vanessa awoke to the sound of a door slamming down the hall, the same door that she had heard many times before, and she knew who it was. She glanced at Shyla, who at first glace looked fine, but when Vanessa looked a little harder she noticed beads of sweat running down her face. "Shyla, are you all right?"

Shyla slowly looked toward Vanessa and tried to focus. "I think it's time."

Vanessa's heart began to race. "What do you mean? You mean now? Oh god." She began to kick against the restraints in a feeble attempt to break free. "Taylor! Taylor! Oh fuck, I have to get out of these shackles. Shyla, it's okay, honey, I'm right here."

Taylor suddenly came around the corner. "Yes, my sweet, what can I do for you?"

Vanessa's panic-stricken face told Taylor what he needed to know. "Shyla is having contractions! Help her!"

Taylor looked at Shyla, beaming. "Wonderful, it won't be long now." He left the room and a moment later came back with a bowl of cold water and a cloth. He began wiping Shyla's head to cool her down and then placed his hand on her protruding belly. He checked the monitors and then turned to Vanessa. "Aren't you lucky, you get to witness a very special birth."

Vanessa's stomach turned slightly at the thought of what exactly she was going to witness. She had no idea what grotesque creature was going to come out of Shyla. At this point all she cared about was keeping Shyla alive. Taylor pushed a couple buttons on the morphine machine beside him. Shyla threw her head back and let out a guttural scream as the contractions increased.

Vanessa tensed. "What the hell are you doing to her?"

Taylor didn't bother to look at Vanessa. "This is going to be a very painful process so I am giving her something for the pain. I'm not completely inhuman, although there's not much I can do for her now. It is all going to happen on its own."

"What the hell do you mean? Can't you give her an epidural or something?"

Taylor laughed. "Sweetheart, that isn't going to take away all the pain that she is about to endure, but I can at least take the edge off. Just watch, observe, and learn. It'll all be over soon. Then I will deal with you."

. . . .

Jim got out of the car and hid in a nearby bush and watched as Taylor walked into the building. He scanned the area to make sure he was alone and then picked up his cell phone again to call Marcus.

"Hey, it's me. I am about five miles out of town. When you are going down the main road you will see a sign that says "JD Holdings." Turn left and follow it down. I am hiding in a bush near the building. Whistle or something to let me know you're near. I'll wait for you." Suddenly he heard a bone-chilling scream. "You better hurry. Something's going down."

Jim hung up and hurried his way around the building to find a window. He stretched on his tiptoes to see inside but couldn't see through the dirty window. He kept walking and found another window that seemed a little cleaner. He also found a crate and pulled it closer. He tested his weight on the old wooden slates, making sure he wouldn't fall through. When he was satisfied, he stood on it and peered inside the building. To the right all he saw were some monitors and computers on a desk. To the left he saw incubation equipment and test tubes.

"What the hell is he doing in there?" He saw a movement on the screen of one of the monitors but couldn't quite make it out. He rubbed the sleeve of his jacket on the widow in an attempt to clean it for a better view. He could make out a woman's body, but it looked distorted. There was a whistle behind him in the distance. Stepping down carefully, he turned and walked back to the bush and looked for Marcus. He saw him waving at him to stay where he was. Marcus crouched down and shuffled his way to Jim's side.

"What did you see?"

Jim sat down on the soft moss-laden ground. "Well, I know this building. It used to belong to my Uncle John on my dad's side of the family. It was an old refinery, but when my uncle died it was given to my father, who never did anything with it and left it to rot. He figured the land was worth more than the building. It's been condemned for years and never used. As for seeing anything, all I could see were a couple of monitors and machines. There is a woman in there, but I can't be sure it was Vanessa. Did you call for backup?"

"Yeah, they're on their way. Did you see if there was anyone with him?"

"Not from what I saw, and there is only one car. He didn't have anyone with him coming out here."

"Good, maybe he was stupid enough to not bring his friend." Marcus looked hopeful.

Jim gazed toward the building. "I don't know what we are going to come across, Marcus. Are you sure you are ready for this?"

There was another scream, and the men jumped. Marcus's eyes widened as he grabbed Jim's arm. "I can't wait for backup. I have to go in. God knows what he is doing to her." Marcus jumped up and ran for the front door. Jim tried to stop him, but Marcus jerked out of his grasp. He cursed under his breath and jumped up and ran after Marcus. They skidded to a halt at the door and pressed their backs up against the wall. Jim grabbed Marcus before he had a chance to go in. "Are you out of your damn mind? We don't know if he has a weapon or not."

Marcus faced Jim. "Don't worry, I have that covered." He reached into his jacket pocket and pulled out a Colt .45 handgun.

Jim shook his head. "Where the hell did you get that! Now is not the time to try to be a hero, Marcus. We have to wait for the police and let them handle it."

There was another blood-curdling scream, and Marcus looked at Jim once more. "I'm going with or without you, Jim."

Reluctantly, Jim nodded. "Okay, fine! On three. One, two, three!" The two men slipped through the door commando style undetected. They crept down the hall and followed the sound of voices. Taylor

Lemay could be heard talking to someone. Jim and Marcus stopped in midstride. Then they heard Vanessa's pleading voice, and Marcus's heart began to beat faster. Only one thought was going through his mind. *Thank god she's alive.*

They began slowly and cautiously walking toward the room Vanessa and Taylor were in. Marcus stopped just outside the doorway and gestured to Jim to go in first. Jim looked around for something to use as a weapon, but the only thing he could come close to was a broom handle. He looked at Marcus and shrugged and mouthed the words, "It's better than nothing."

Marcus slowly moved the plastic to the side and jumped inside, gun raised.

"Stop right there, Taylor! Don't make a move or I'll blow you motherfucking head off!"

Taylor jumped and Vanessa screamed. Jim went to grab Taylor when the sight of Shyla caught his eye. "What the hell—"

Taylor took the opportunity to grab the broomstick from Jim's hand and swung it at his head. It connected with a crack, and Jim flew into the wall. He slid to the floor. Taylor lunged at Marcus in a football tackle, and the gun was knocked from Marcus's hand as he hit the floor. Taylor grabbed Marcus's shirt and swung to punch him in the face, but Marcus recoiled to seize the arm that was coming toward him at lightning speed. The two men kicked and lashed at each other wildly.

Jim started to get his bearings again and struggled to his feet. Blood trickled down the side of his head. His hairline began to mat with the thick red fluid. Marcus was on top of Taylor with his arm across his throat holding him down. As Taylor thrashed trying to free himself, Marcus reached for the gun, which was just out of his grasp. "Jim! Get the gun!"

Jim looked toward Marcus's outstretched hand and saw what he was reaching for. With the gun in his shaky hands he pointed it at the two men. "I got it! Marcus, get off him. I got him covered!"

Marcus held Taylor in place long enough so he could get up without giving Taylor the advantage. "You move and you're dead, you hear me?"

Taylor put his hand up in surrender, let Marcus get up, and then looked at Jim. "How did you figure out it was me?"

Jim tried to steady his hands. "That's not important."

Marcus went to Vanessa's side. "Are you okay? Did he hurt you?" He struggled with the shackles but couldn't open them. He saw the IV that was attached to her. He looked in her eyes. "I have to take this out."

Vanessa nodded and took a deep breath as Marcus pulled the long needle from her body. Then he kissed her gently on the forehead.

Vanessa began to cry. "What took you so long? I thought I was dead for sure."

Marcus kissed her again. "I'll explain everything later, but right now I have to get you out of here." Marcus looked at Jim, who was dumbstruck at the sight he had before him. "Jim! Get the key for the shackles!"

Jim turned to Taylor, who in turn looked back stunned. "Where are the keys?"

Taylor pointed to his pocket. "I have them."

Jim motioned for Taylor to hand them over, and Taylor did so reluctantly.

"I'm actually glad you are here. Now we can witness this together."

Jim reached for the ring of keys and tossed them to Marcus. "What the hell are you doing to her, Taylor?"

Taylor relaxed despite the gun aimed at his head. "Well, before I tell you that, I want to tell you a little story that you might be interested in."

Jim glared at him in disgust. "I don't have time for your stories, damn it. I asked you a question."

Taylor chuckled. "You have no idea who I am, do you?"

Jim spat the words out. "I know that you are a spoiled little rich kid whose number is up!"

Taylor's eyes narrowed. "Look a little closer ... Dad."

Jim's jaw dropped, and Marcus suddenly turned to look at them.

"You bastard! What games do you think you're playing? I don't have a child."

Taylor turned toward him. "Oh, really, guess what. You're wrong. You know my mother all too well. Her name is Lydia Lemay, but you knew her as Lydia Perez of Perez Manor."

The blood drained from Jim's face and he stumbled back. "No."

"Oh yes. You see, after you raped her, she found out she was

149

pregnant with me. She fled Peru so her father wouldn't find out. But guess what. He did, and he disowned her because she wouldn't have an abortion. Of course, being as high-classed as the Perez were, he would be damned if he was going to have his daughter keep the baby of the man who took advantage of her. How would that look to his peers? So, she lost her inheritance and her family, all because of you."

Taylor's eyes shifted to Shyla. "So I thought to myself, what better way to avenge my mother's pain and suffering than to come back to Peru and have my father teach me everything he knows about entomology and biology and take away his brass ring."

The confusion on Jim's face made Taylor feel victorious knowing he got the reaction he wanted.

Jim tried to absorb all the information that Taylor laid out for him, but the shock of it all wouldn't allow him to speak.

When Jim said nothing, Taylor continued. "I found out about your little experiment, Daddy dear, but I changed it a little. While you were the good humanitarian and injecting yourself with the DNA, I was injecting myself as well. All I needed was the spider DNA from your precious spider, but that was easy. I also took it upon myself to abstract some of her eggs so I could grow my own super-species."

Taylor cautiously stood up and pointed to the glass aquarium in the corner of the room. "Let me introduce you to Minerva."

The massive spider stood up on her back legs and stretched up the side of the glass. Her black coat shone in the florescent lighting, and her fangs dripped toxic venom. Taylor smiled at his perfect specimen. "Her breed is a little different than your prized Lydia. She is a cross between the Brazilian wandering spider, which as you know is the most venomous spider in the world, the brown recluse, which also can painfully shut down the nervous system killing you in fifteen minutes, and of course, last but not least, the Goliath bird-eater tarantula, which is the biggest tarantula in the world."

He tapped his index finger on his chin. "So I guess you could say she is Lydia's daughter. After all that, I had to find a match for the incubation process. I tried to let Minerva find her own host, but that proved to be a little messy. She is the one that killed all those villagers. I guess she knew they had something wrong with them and promptly killed them instead of planting her eggs in them, so I had to look for one myself." A broad smile crossed Taylor's face. "Granted, I had to go through a couple girls and had a little fun along the way, but hey, what can I say. I'm a chip off the old block."

Shyla moaned in the background as Taylor excitedly finished the story. "I searched for a couple years as I traveled all over the world, but to no avail. Then I found her in my own home town, go figure." He turned toward Shyla and winked. "Of course I had to let your little eight-legged friend go so your side of the project couldn't be finished, and without the spider you had nothing. Shyla's blood type and genetic makeup were perfect for the incubation process."

Marcus struggled to free Vanessa from the prison that held her for day after agonizing day. He looked up at her and saw the terror-filled look on her face. Her face contorted into a painful grimace, her eyes grew wide, and tears streamed down her cheeks.

Vanessa looked at Taylor with growing hate. "We have to get Shyla to a hospital."

Taylor smiled. "A hospital can't help her anymore." He pointed toward Shyla.

A deep throaty scream reverberated off the walls, and all eyes turned to Shyla's battered body. Her naked, pregnant frame hung on the wall, muscles stiff and shaking. Her head was thrown back in an unnatural position with her neck extended as far as it could go.

Taylor turned to Jim. "I'm glad we had this talk, Dad. It means so much that you are going to witness this special occasion with me. You are about to see the third generation be born."

Jim's stomach turned as he looked at Shyla, and then he mumbled under his breath, "There is no way in hell I could produce such a malicious offspring!"

Vanessa stepped back and grabbed on to Marcus, and he in turn took his jacket off, wrapping it around her shaking body, and then instinctively put his arms around her.

Shyla moaned in agony as her stomach began to stretch and move. Her eyes suddenly closed tight, and a gurgling scream escaped her lips as she turned to look at Vanessa. "Help me!"

Shyla's amniotic sac broke, and the reddish yellow fluid burst, splashing all over the floor. Vomit spewed from her mouth as a grotesque cracking sound came from her pelvic bone as it broke in pieces.

Shyla's screams were deafening, and there was nothing anyone could do but watch in horror as every blood vessel began to burst. Her body arched back as every vertebra in her spine compressed within her body. The skin suddenly stretched until it gave way as the stomach lining began to rip open under the pressure.

Jim's body began to revolt as he heaved out the lunch that he had eaten and was now a puddle on the floor. He steadied himself on the wall, unable to watch the grotesque scene any longer.

Blood began to pour from Shyla's vaginal cavity as she started choking violently on the steady flow of vomit that escaped her swollen lips. Blood sprayed and gushed in all directions causing the group to jump back.

Shyla's body began to spasm, and Vanessa sobbed. To the revulsion of everyone except Taylor, Shyla's torn stomach gave way to a sea of baby spiders that began to crawl out of the now-quivering cavity of what used to be a beautiful woman.

The hundreds of baby spiders fought to be the first ones born as they scattered all along her corpse in search of the mother that was not there.

Taylor's insane laughter hung in the room like a thick fog. Marcus grabbed Vanessa's hand. "Come on, let's get out of here. There's nothing we can do for her now. The police will be outside soon." Vanessa took one more look at the shattered remains of a woman who had her whole life ahead of her.

Shyla's lifeless body now hung as a monument and testament to the sick reality of the world around them. Vanessa's tears streamed down her face. Her eyes were puffy and red. Feeling defeated and helpless, she put her head down and started walking out the door followed by Marcus.

Suddenly, the same cold chill that hit Vanessa in the university office hit her again. She felt the same presence she had felt before and knew what it was as she scanned the room. Marcus stopped and squeezed her hand reassuringly. "What's wrong?" He followed her gaze, trying to focus on the spot she was looking at.

There on the ceiling above Taylor Lemay's head was the expectant grandmother watching over the babies as they entered the world.

Taylor glared at Marcus and Vanessa. "What the hell are you looking at?"

Marcus put his arm around Vanessa, guided her out the door, and then turned to smile at Taylor, who was pointed to the ceiling. "I do believe you have a visitor." Jim and Taylor looked up, and Jim stumbled backward toward the doorway and smiled.

"Lydia."

Taylor had a disinterested look as he began to look up at the ceiling. "What the hell are you talking …" His words trailed off as his eyes connected with Lydia's. Her eight-inch frame radiated her splendor and grace. Her blue coat shone against the bright lights as the realization of Taylor's fate became apparent on his face. A blood-curdling scream escaped Taylor as Lydia expelled her large body down over Taylor's shock-stricken body.

Before he even had a chance to fight her, Lydia sunk her fangs through his collar and into Taylor's skin. She released thick venom that would render him motionless. Taylor felt the paralysis seize his body and had no choice but to give in to his predator as his body crashed to the floor.

Lydia moved swiftly, crawling under his shirt and placing her body at Taylor's pectoral muscle, knowing this would be a good anchor, and sunk her eight legs deep into the flesh. Her barbed feet secured her body as the cobalt beauty began to suck the life out of her victim.

Jim slowly walked toward the back storage room and found what he was looking for. He lifted the jerrycan and began spreading the fluid all around the room.

Out of love for Lydia DeMone, Jim's decision to destroy the evidence was an easy one. He couldn't bare the thought that she would find out what a monster their son had become. Even more, he couldn't live with the fact that it was him who indirectly created that monster. Once he was finished, he reached into his pocket and pulled out the matchbook.

He took one more look at his son and Lydia. Remorse filled his heart as he lit the match. He threw it into the middle of the room and turned to walk away, not realizing his boot was entangled on the cords to the machines that were attached to Shyla's corpse. He looked down and struggled to get the cords loosened, but the more he pulled, the tighter they got.

A wall of flames shot up in front of him, singeing his face. He tried to run, but the weight of the machine held him in his place as he fell forward onto the gasoline that was now spreading across the floor.

He struggled to get his boot off his foot, but the flames engulfed him before he had the chance to get it loose.

Lydia squealed as the flames charred her vibrant hair and the fire took her life.

As the last breath left Jim, his final thought was of the cruel irony that all took place when he interfered with Mother Nature's creation in hopes to build a new species that would exceed the life span of most spiders, therefore diverting the arachnid species continuum for the better good of a dying breed. Mother Nature, in turn, reminded Jim Dunstan, Taylor Lemay, that things happen for a reason and to leave well enough alone.

While most animals spread their sperm in water or insert them into the female, male spiders have a secondary copulatory organ, so male spiders weave a small web. They place a drop of semen on the web, suck it up with their pedipalps, and then use the pedipalps to insert the sperm into a female.

Chapter 19

It was a warm afternoon with the sun shinning brightly over the graveyard. A slight breeze carried the sweet scent of Heliconia blossoms that made Marcus smile.

The priest finished the eulogy, placed the earth on the caskets, and pressed his Bible to his chest. "Ashes to ashes, dust to dust."

Vanessa watched as a woman clad in black, with a black veil hiding her face, walked up to the casket closest to her and placed a shaking hand on the polished mahogany. Her voice cracked as she tried to speak through the steady stream of tears. "Sleep well, my son."

The team followed behind the procession as they led their way over to the grieving mother to say their condolences. Vanessa led the team first. "You must be Lydia."

The woman gazed through the veil numbly. "And you must be Vanessa." Vanessa's shocked expression didn't surprise the woman. "My son wasn't always the angel I gave birth to, but he was my only son and I love him very much. I understand why he did the things I was told, but he never knew the whole story and that was my fault."

Her thick Peruvian accent took on a solemn tone. "I never thought that he would have set out to find his father. Now they are both gone."

Vanessa reached out to take the woman's hand, but Lydia pulled away and then asked, "He hurt you, didn't he? You don't have to answer that. I already know. It came to me in a vision, a horrible nightmare."

She turned to walk away. "I'm so sorry for the pain Taylor caused you." Then she walked away with her husband beside her.

Vanessa turned to Marcus with a painful expression on her face. He took her hand, and the team walked through the maze of headstones.

When they reached the car, a voice broke the grizzly silence. "Dr. Tolson, wait!" A tall man jogged down the path toward them holding a folder in his hand.

"Countess Lemay wanted you to have this. She said you could do what you wish with it."

Marcus took the folder. "What is it?" He opened it.

"That is not for me to know, sir. That is between you and the countess." He turned on his heels and walked away.

Marcus got in the car and opened it carefully. The note attached to the inside was addressed to him personally. It read:

> Dr. Tolson,
> I received this file the day after Jim Dunstan and my son died. Jim must have asked his lawyer to send it in the case of his untimely death.
> It talks about the experiment that he was working on as well as why he felt he needed to do it.
> It seems that his guilt over what happened between him and myself many years ago overtook his soul. Therefore, he felt he was indebted to me in some way.
> He named his experiment Lydia after me and, upon the success of the experiment, was going to dedicate that success to me.
> He always was a foolish man. I have no need for these papers, but I thought you might have some interest in them.
> If in the case you proceed with his work, I would appreciate it if you changed the name, as I don't need the constant reminder of all that has happened.
> Regards,
> Countess Lydia Lemay

Marcus closed the file and handed it to Vanessa. The team quietly got into the Land Rover, and for the first time they didn't bicker and fight. Randy sat with a frown on his face, trying to understand the events of the past week. Larry helped Vanessa into the front passenger seat and then squished in beside a pale-looking Cliff. The team sat quietly for a few moments, not sure if they should say anything.

Vanessa gave Marcus a probing look, hoping he would give her some insight into the letter he just read. Instead, he took a deep breath, turned the key in the ignition, put the car in drive, and began the long drive to the airport.

The huntsman spider often gets confused with the tarantula because of its body frame and hair. It is not considered a dangerous spider and is reluctant to bite; rather, it will run from humans.

Epilogue

"Push, Vanessa. Come on, you can do it!" The nurse held Vanessa's right leg into position as Marcus tried to do the same on the left. The baby's head crowned, and Vanessa put every possible ounce of energy into the final push, the sweat soaked sheets grasped firmly in her hands as a groan escaped her lips.

Marcus looked down as the new addition entered the world with eyes wide open. Marcus's eyes began to tear as he laid his eyes on the most beautiful child he had ever seen.

Vanessa's exhausted body relaxed against the bed as she gazed upon their beautiful son. The doctor removed the mucus from the baby's mouth and nose and then handed him to the nurse. She wrapped him in the soft knitted blue blanket that Vanessa spent most of her pregnancy making and then handed him to the elated new mother.

"Oh god, Marc, he's so tiny." She smiled up at Marcus.

"Yeah, but he's a Tolson, don't forget. He doesn't need height; he has brains." Marcus smiled down at Vanessa and kissed her forehead.

Vanessa looked down at the little face looking back at her. "I want you to meet someone, Alexander. This is your daddy."

Vanessa handed the bundle to her shaky husband. He held the child in his arms and sat down beside Vanessa on the bed, and she reached over to wipe a tear from his cheek.

"Wow, we have been waiting for you for a long time, kiddo. Welcome to the first day of the rest of your life." He touched the tiny hand that reached out to him. "I promise to protect you from all the bad habits your mom tries to teach you when she is on all those PMS days. And oh, man, I'll teach you to run when she makes you meatloaf." Marcus scrunched up his face in protest.

Vanessa laughed and jabbed him in the arm. The doctor and nurses left the room, leaving the couple to enjoy their time together.

An hour later, Vanessa slept peacefully as Marcus sat in the rocking chair with baby Alexander cooing softly in his arms.

Marcus chuckled as an unpleasant smell escaped the blanket. "Whew, you really are your mother's son, aren't you? Don't tell her I said that."

Marcus stood up, walked to the changing table, and laid the child down. He grabbed a diaper from the basket to his left and whispered his confession to his newborn son. "I hope I remember how to do this. I have to be honest and tell you that I was the diaper changing champ in our Lamaze class. Your mother was so proud. She tried to take credit for teaching me everything she knows, but I think the teacher saw through it. I'm just a natural diaper-changing, poop-wiping, spittle-catching type of guy."

He removed the blanket and unfastened the jumper suit carefully, making sure not to pinch Alexander's skin. He found the tape on either side that held the diaper together and removed one at a time, pulling back the folds carefully.

Suddenly, the breath caught in Marcus's throat and his hands began to shake.

In the cotton fibers of the diaper lay strand upon strand of webbing that clung to the baby's thighs, scrotum, and penis.

Marcus's heart raced beyond its limits. He opened his mouth to yell, but nothing came out. Staggering backward, he knocked over the bassinet that sat beside the bed and fell to the floor. The pain became unbearable as he clutched his chest. He reached up, clawing at the bed in the attempt to wake his sleeping beauty.

Vanessa woke with a start. "Marcus! My god, what's wrong?" She pushed the nurses button that lay beside her, got out of the bed, and went to his side.

Marcus's heart slowed as his scared eyes looked up at the woman he loved with every inch of his being.

He tried to speak one last time. "Alex—" Then his heart stopped, and the room gave way to a sea of black as he exhaled his final breath.

His body went limp in Vanessa's arms as two nurses came through the door. The one nurse pulled Vanessa to her feet and started CPR on Marcus, and the other nurse yelled down the hall, "Code blue! Get the crash cart down here stat!"

Vanessa scanned the room for Alexander and walked quickly to the baby that lay on the changing table. She looked down at the cooing child in horror as she realized what Marcus was trying to tell her. Tears rolled down her face as she lifted her son off the table and rocked him in her arms and then weakly crumbled to the floor.

"No, not you." Her arm tightened around the child as she hugged him close to her. Through uncontrollable tears and a broken heart, she kissed her baby on the forehead. "I will always love you, my precious son."

She looked at the nurses working on Marcus and then back at Alexander. "Please forgive me."

Vanessa laid the baby on her lap and gently placed her hands on the child's face, covering his nose and mouth. "I'm so sorry."

After what seemed like an eternity, Alexander lay motionless in her arms as if he was sleeping peacefully. The reality of what she had done sunk deep within Vanessa's spirit. Her screams and sobs could be heard throughout the hospital ward as Vanessa's unfathomable cries escaped her soul.

Printed in the United States
By Bookmasters